MOON AND STARS

ELIZABETH JOHNS

For those who do not fit the mold

CHAPTER 1

It is quite liberating. I have reached an age when I am not mooning for romance and can be my own person. I can safely pronounce I am in no danger of making myself ridiculous for the elusive emotion called love.—Lady Charlotte 21 Dec

*I*t was always someone else's wedding, Lady Charlotte Stanton thought as she stood alone on the terrace, looking up at the dark, starry night. She had reached the age where she could be as improper as she liked and people would only shake their heads and call her eccentric. Part of her wished it were true. In reality, she spent most of her evenings in front of a warm fire, curled up with a Minerva Press novel and a few cats to keep her company. It was not a bad life. It was often preferable to having to engage superficially with humans who expected witty repartee.

Nevertheless, there were those times when even she craved touch —human touch—and wondered what it would feel like to be kissed and held in adoration by someone she loved. Jealousy was not the precise emotion she felt, but there had been scores of love matches amongst her family and friends, and she was perhaps, on occasion, envious. It did not lessen her joy and delight for them by any means.

Earlier that day she had witnessed the union of the Duke of Cavenray to Maili Craig. She was not directly related, but she had formed a friendship with the bride on a visit to London in the spring. Maili, too, had always felt an outsider but had managed to find love. Charlotte stared up at the stars and could not help but wonder if there was more for her, somewhere out there.

"Sometimes I think I have more in common with the moon and the stars than Polite Society," a deep, baritone voice said from behind her, as if the man had heard her thoughts.

Charlotte managed not to flinch. She was unused to anyone seeking her company in dark places.

"Yes, I was brought up amongst the *ton*, yet it is not often comfortable," she replied, still looking at the night sky.

"That is the last word I would use for it," he said as he came to stand next to her. He was so close she felt warmth radiating from him and smelt his scent of spice and pine. She was afraid to turn and look. She did not wish to ruin the moment with reality, yet the arm of his coat appeared to be well made, and his hands appeared to be strong.

They stood there in silent kinship, listening to the sounds of laughter and dancing coming from the ballroom.

"Would you care to dance?"

Charlotte did not answer. This man must be someone new in Town, someone who knew not who she was, or could not see her clearly in the moonlight. What did it matter? It was only a dance. One dance would change nothing.

She held her hand out to him and finally allowed herself to look up.

"Have we been introduced?" she asked, annoyed at her inanity. She had never before seen this man, of that she was certain.

His light grey eyes twinkled in the moonlight, and they were looking at her—her!—flirtatiously. Crinkles formed at the edges of his eyes, indicating an experience and maturity that made him more handsome when he smiled. It was devilish cruel that men became more striking with age.

"You know very well we have not," he answered.

He pulled her close—too close—and began to twirl her around. The moment was too intimate for mere words. Charlotte felt light and dainty for the first time ever as this man spun her in his arms. She must be dreaming. It was a heady, delicious feeling as her pulse raced and her insides quivered.

When the music ceased, they stood there still, retaining the position of the dance as their breathing slowed. Charlotte grew self-conscious as the man studied her.

"Am I to know your name?" she whispered.

He took her hand and brought it to his lips, sending shivers through her.

"Some things are better left unspoken, my lady." He looked down at her, a hint of self-derision etched in the features of his face. She wanted to capture everything about this moment, for surely she would soon wake, and she wished to remember it: The clear midnight sky twinkling with stars, the crescent moon, the sound of horses clopping by intermingled with crickets chirping, his unusual scent wafting on the warm breeze…

"You have the advantage of me, sir. That is not very gentlemanly." Their eyes met and she could not look away. The icy grey eyes hinted at danger, yet she felt safe in his arms.

"Ah, but I am no gentleman."

"I do not believe you."

"What gentleman would approach a lady alone on a dark terrace?" As if his words made him realize he was still holding her, he took a step back and released her.

Immediately, she felt the loss of warmth and the chill night air. "I could state any number of instances I have observed over the past decade. Unfortunately, none of them included myself," Charlotte retorted, wondering why she was being so bold. She could see his lips twitch, then break into a smile, at her reply. If he was attractive before, he was sinfully handsome when he smiled. "However, if you were not a gentleman you would not be here amongst my friends. You are familiar yet why do I not know you?"

"I am not surprised you do not remember me. I have lived abroad for some time. I longed for my homeland, but now that I am here I do not know if it is possible for me to belong again."

"I am the last person to give advice on belonging," she whispered while simultaneously searching her memories for this man.

His face looked up with interest. "Do you have regrets, my lady?"

"Nothing so delicious as to be called regrets—more like disappointments," she added.

"And I would hesitate to call mine regrets—more like dishonour and disgrace."

"It cannot be so horrid, or you would not be standing here a free man," she argued.

He hesitated as church bells sounded in the distance. "Unfortunately, I may not be so for long. I should leave you before my presence taints your good name."

"There is little you could do to hurt my reputation, I am afraid."

He stepped closer and ran the back of his hand gently down her face. "If only it were true."

A shiver went down her spine. His dark, bold looks tempted her to abandon all good sense. "I was long ago relegated to the hopeless list, sir. No one notices when I escape for fresh air. I seldom dance—I am allowed to *chaperone,* for goodness sake!" Her fists balled at her sides and she longed to pound them against something to relieve her frustration.

"You are anything but hopeless," he murmured in husky tones, making her heart skip a beat.

"I have never even been kissed, sir." Why had she uttered her ultimate humiliation? It was something she would wonder later as he cradled her face with his other hand and lowered his lips to meet hers. She gasped with surprise as she tried to comprehend the new sensations of someone else's lips on hers and make sense of the liquid heat pulsing through her veins. It was enough to disorder her wits. As she leaned into the kiss and allowed her hands to lightly touch his chest, she wanted to remember every moment so she could savour this forever. It was very different from her imaginings—tender yet carnal. His lips moved to caress both cheeks before he gently pulled away.

"Why did you do that? You need not indulge my self-pity," she chastised without heat when she came to her senses, turning sharply to hide her mortification.

"I never indulge pity. A kiss is the only thing I have to offer you."

"I refuse to believe you." She felt an instant connection to him that she did not understand. Never before could she have spoken to someone so openly. Normally she had to repress a babbling, silly tongue around people for whom she felt attraction. She could not countenance the idea her intuition would misguide her so. "I still cannot understand what you think so awful it would be unforgivable. You do have a bit of the look of a rogue about you, but so do half of the men beyond those doors." She indicated the terrace doors with a flick of her wrist.

"Rogue is one word that has been used to describe me."

"I can also imagine you were a bit of a rapscallion in your youth, pilfering fresh biscuits and apple tarts from Cook."

"I did not have to pilfer them," he said with a twinkle in his eye from the moonlight.

"I can also envision you as a rake-hell just down from University. Again, a trait most of the gentleman in the ballroom share." She waved her hand dismissively.

"Ah, my lady, but should you put all of those together, with the arrogance and pride of youth combined with lack of title or estates, and you come up with a very dangerous equation." He looked at her with what she could only term as regret as he bowed over her hand and pressed his lips to her palm in one final intimate caress. "Take care, my lady."

"Please do not leave me," she whispered, but he did not hear.

He walked away, his boots echoing on the flagstones, leaving her behind on the terrace to stare longingly after him. Her lips were still warm from his. She felt like the prince left behind at the stroke of midnight, except she had no glass slipper with which to trace him.

～

DAVID CURSED himself as he escaped from Lady Charlotte Stanton and the ball. The rogue in him had toyed with throwing her over his shoulder and abducting her. How could he forget himself so? He had admired her from afar, and his feet had followed her seemingly of their own volition onto the terrace. Remarkably, she was still unwed. Had the bucks in London no sense? Or did she have too much intelligence to accept any of them? In all likelihood, it was the latter, he decided. Lady Charlotte was beautiful, but she had a confidence about her which made her irresistible. There was something decidedly more appealing about a woman who knew her own mind and was at ease with herself. Her thick blonde locks threatening to burst from their pins, her voluptuous curves in all the right places, and a touch of irreverence in her manner, tempted him as no other of the fair sex had done. Then those large, green eyes had looked at him pleadingly —he found he could not resist her. For that reason alone, he should board a ship and return to the West Indies—if he was still a free man when the King had finished with him.

Stepping out onto Grafton Street with one last glance at the luxurious town house alight with the private celebration of the Cavenray wedding, he shook his head at his audacity. He was happy to see his niece, Maili, find happiness with the Duke, but being here was a sharp reminder of how far he had fallen—not that he had ever been lofty enough for a Duke's daughter. He was only the prodigal younger son of a baronet.

There was wretched irony in that he had returned to England a wealthy man, and it was to be forever shadowed by his past. Lord Brennan had resumed his threats the moment David had set foot back in England. Fortunately the truth had won out and Brennan had paid the ultimate price for his sins, but it did not mean there would be no more punishment for his own youthful follies.

His future was at the mercy of Prinny, now King George IV. Cavenray said he was certain the King would pardon David when he learned all the sordid details of Brennan's involvement in the exposed smuggling scheme. David was not so confident. Over a decade ago, he had not minded his self-imposed exile. Now, he longed to settle and grow old in his native land. No longer Sir David—he never actually was the legitimate baronet—he had only acted as steward over that land from afar for his nephew, Seamus. The power and title he had once envied enough to betray his honourable name was no longer enticing, but Lady Charlotte was. He was not for the likes of her.

Even if he received a pardon, he would never be accepted by Polite Society or as her equal. Rumours abounded of his involvement in Brennan's smuggling ring; even if half of them were true, he had been given credit for all of it. It was time to retreat to the shadows for good, where he belonged.

~

YARDLEY WATCHED the doors until the unknown gentleman reappeared after quite a lengthy time outside, alone with Charlotte. The man then escaped from Cavenray House as though the hounds of hell were at his feet—as if he had known Yardley was waiting to confront him.

"Who was the gentleman I espied dancing on the terrace with my sister?" Yardley asked Cavenray discreetly when he finally reached that gentleman's side amongst the crowd. He had noticed Charlotte slipping from the ballroom, but by the time he made to join her outside, he had found her waltzing in the arms of an unknown man. Quashing his initial response to throttle the gentleman, he realized it behoved him to discover his identity rather than place his sister in scandal's path. He had remained inside the door to make certain no one else discovered the couple.

"I did not see anyone on the terrace, I am afraid," Cavenray said, his amusement betrayed by the light in his eyes.

"While I appreciate your discretion, I do not wish for my sister to be hurt. She is more sensitive than her careless manner would suggest," Yardley said with feeling.

"Then I suppose we should find a more private place for this discussion." He led him to his private study in the back corner of the house, and handed him a drink before they settled in armchairs near the fire.

Yardley was not pleased when Cavenray explained his history with David Douglas—Captain Deuce—and his plan to plead for pardon from the King on Douglas' behalf. The man had been a smuggler, kidnapper and murderer by repute, regardless of the why of it. Douglas was related to the Craig family, who was Yardley's family by marriage. Yet he could not abide the idea of his sister becoming involved with a criminal. He would have to determine a way to keep this man from Charlotte, even if she had looked beautiful and happy for the first time he could remember since her come out. He would have to make certain she never found out.

CHAPTER 2

The world stood still for me last evening, although I still do not know whether I imagined the whole. Tall, dark and handsome goes the saying, but what is never mentioned are the sensations and fragrances. I shall forever remember the strange scent of spice mixed with pine, and the feel of his strong, warm hands on me. Was there ever more pleasure on earth than when two pairs of lips first meet? Suddenly I feel as though I have tasted the forbidden fruit.
—22 Dec

Charlotte felt changed. If she had known what a kiss would feel like, she might have exerted herself more when she was younger. It had been nothing like those she had dreamed about, and she had imagined kisses with several gentlemen. She had never been comfortable when gentleman drew close.

It would not have been so simple to steal kisses, of course. Chaperones guarded a girl's every move when she was just out, but somehow, once she neared the ripe old age of eight and twenty, no one worried for her virtue any longer. Apparently, age was its own chaperone.

Not that she had ever found anyone worth exerting herself for, she reminded herself. The only interested parties had been either too old, wanted her wealth and family name, or were too fashionable for her comfort. No one had really wanted *her*.

She was certain everyone would know by looking at her what she had been doing on the terrace the night before but, as usual, no one had even noticed her absence. Her heart beat faster this morning, and she felt different. Knowing. Educated. Mature. Feeling her cheeks burn while recalling her own boldness, she let a laugh escape. It felt glorious.

Throwing back the coverlet, she was excited to begin her new life as she placed her feet on the lush carpet. She felt giddy about her future... until she sat down at her dressing table and looked at her reflection. Then the doubts crept in. Ridiculous and self-pitying, she remembered she did not even know the handsome stranger's name. Who could he be? He seemed to know her, but she was quite, quite certain she would not have forgotten him.

Picking up her grandmother's old hairbrush, she ran it through her locks mindlessly as she reflected. She was well beyond her first bloom, if she had ever had one, and polite people referred to her as healthy—certainly not the latest mode of wispy and thin. Once, her friend Lady Olivia had given her hope of being attractive enough to make a match, but Charlotte's figure had made her much too shy to entice anyone except the desperate. Before she had overcome her shyness, she was firmly on the shelf. Collecting dust.

At least, now, she could die having been kissed. It would have to do.

Everyone had long ago accepted her spinsterhood—as had she, yet the dark, handsome stranger called to her inner longing. He made the contentment she had only thought she had achieved now feel like a drab, unpleasant state of existence. Charlotte never did anything exciting or unexpected. Did anyone truly know her? The longing to do something more bold filled her heart.

Charlotte was one of the last down to breakfast. She did not particularly enjoy early morning without a good reason. Everyone else had eaten and were preparing to return to their country estates that day. Only her brother and his wife, Jolie, remained in the breakfast parlour.

"Good morning, Lottie," her brother greeted her as he set down his cup of coffee.

"Good morning, Benedict. Jolie." She could not help but smile this morning despite her self-doubt. Even the bright yellow room echoed her sunny disposition today.

"Are you feeling quite the thing, Lottie? You seem different," Jolie asked with a suspicious glance of her violet eyes.

"I feel quite well, thank you," she replied in the most unassuming manner she could manage as she made her way to the mahogany sideboard to fill her plate.

"Charlotte, we were just talking about you and wondering if you would care to come to Yardley with us? Since Mother is away in Italy, I cannot abide the thought of you going back to Langdon House alone."

"Benedict, I think it is high time you stop thinking of me as a schoolroom chit and accept I am past my prayers. No one will think anything of it. Besides, you know how I loathe winter and it is harsh enough on the south coast." She placed some bacon and eggs on her plate with deliberate slowness before turning around to face the conversation she dreaded.

"Then I insist you find a companion." He flashed his determined, green-eyed look at her which he tended to do when issuing ducal edicts. She would not be dictated to in this.

"Do not be ridiculous. Mother will return soon, and I have my maid until then. No one will take note either way. I never go into local society." She placed her plate on the table and sat in one of the large chairs as far away from him as she could.

Her brother let out a loud sigh, which expressed the constant argument they had had over the years. He was quiet while he was gathering his thoughts…she could see by the way he put down his cup and looked at her with pity in his eyes, though she was unprepared for his next question.

"Lottie, are you happy?"

She did not answer for a moment as she tried to quell her anger. However, as she thought about it, she realized she was not happy. Perhaps her experience the night before had made her recognize she was not even content.

"I do not think I could lay claim to happiness precisely," she answered quietly as she plucked a slice of toast from the rack before her and spread butter on it before she took a bite.

"Then why not do something about it?"

"What do you suppose I can do, Benedict? Ladies cannot stroll into White's. I cannot go to the theatre or Astley's or Tattersall's by myself without being thought fast. I cannot be a wife and mother because no one wishes to have me. Is that what you want to hear? The cold, ugly truth?"

She looked up to see her brother and sister-in-law staring at her. Never before had she spoken in such a way to either of them. She continued.

"No, it is much easier to assume the role of plump spinster who stays in the shadows in Society, and jolly aunt to my scores of nieces and nephews. My novels and cats keep me company in the cold winter and do not complain."

Benedict's spoon slid from his hand, the clink echoing in the room.

Jolie finally spoke. "Is there anything else that would make you happy? Helping at one of the schools or orphanages? Travelling? Or do you really wish to be a wife and mother?"

"It would be easier if I knew what I did want. I had always thought I would have children, but there has never been an acceptable opportunity. Perhaps there is something more I could do with my life, though." She pondered this idea.

"We only wish to help, not criticize. I have not been a proper brother in seeing to your future. Is there anyone at all who interests you? Perhaps something could be contrived to put you in the way of some desirable suitors." Charlotte could see her brother's mind taking hold of the idea.

"It is rather too late for me, I am afraid." As she spoke the words, she realized she did not want them to be true.

"With your beauty, fortune and connections, I cannot imagine there would not be some good matches for you," Jolie said, her eyes kind.

Charlotte scoffed and pulled a mocking face. Jolie—the *ton's* most celebrated, goddess-like creature alive—was calling her a beauty? It was too much. She still could not stop the heat she felt coming to her cheeks, though. Charlotte was interested in a man for the first time in her life and she had no idea who he was. It was not something she wished to confess at the breakfast table. "There were some people I was unacquainted with at the ball last night," she confessed, her eyes averted to her tea cup, hoping they would see it as a change of subject.

"I did not see anyone who was not close friends and family. I wonder who it could be? Was it a gentleman?" Jolie asked with undisguised interest.

"Perhaps I have just forgotten," Charlotte remarked, not wanting to draw more notice to the fact. She was often in her own world and did not pay as much attention as she ought.

"Are you well acquainted with David Douglas?" Yardley asked his wife.

"Sir David?" Jolie asked as she reached for the marmalade. "He is Maili's uncle. I only saw a glimpse of him last evening."

"He was not at the ball long," Yardley remarked.

Sir David. Charlotte did not know the name. Could he be her mysterious gentleman?

"Perhaps he is not comfortable in Society yet. Apparently, he was involved in the scandal with Lord Brennan. I heard he was the one who finally brought him to justice," Jolie said after a sip of tea.

Charlotte wanted to know more.

"It does not change the fact of his being a smuggler and kidnapper," Yardley retorted.

Charlotte swallowed her hot tea too fast and tried not to choke.

"Brennan was blackmailing Sir David to gain his assistance. He escaped to the West Indies after Brennan killed several people and placed the blame on him. It is said Brennan killed David's brother and wife, although David managed to save the children. That is how

Seamus, Catriona and Maili came to be at the orphanage where Lord Craig found them," Jolie explained.

Is this why her gentleman had said he was better not to be known? He sounded more like a hero than a scoundrel to her.

"Our departure will be delayed a while. Cavenray has asked me to help him with a small matter this morning." He folded up his paper and set it aside.

"How does he wish for you to help?" Jolie asked, a slight wrinkle forming between her brows.

"To lend my support to having Sir David pardoned. I am well acquainted with dear George."

"Why does he need a pardon if he was innocent?" Charlotte could not help asking.

"He was not completely innocent in his younger days. He was a smuggler," Yardley muttered.

"Will you help?"

"I have yet to decide. I will go along and hear it out. There might be more to the story than I am aware of."

"So long as we can leave today, husband. We must be at Yardley in time for Christmas Eve."

"I will bid you farewell and Season's Greetings now, then. I am off as soon as my trunks are loaded." Charlotte said, wanting to ask more, but she was afraid to expose her interest. If he really was a rogue, it was likely he considered it a game to kiss every pathetic spinster he happened upon. She suddenly felt very sorry for herself and made her excuses to leave the table. It was better to go back to her comfortable way of life where last night's kiss would be but a fond memory.

"WHAT IS GOING ON? Why are you reluctant to help a member of the family?" Jolie asked her husband once Charlotte had departed.

"Can a man not guard his own reputation?" Yardley asked, mildly affronted.

Jolie narrowed her eyes and waited for a proper response.

"Very well. I saw Douglas and Charlotte dancing—waltzing—on the terrace last night."

"How romantic! Were you afraid they would be caught? As Charlotte pointed out, she is rather firmly on the shelf. No one even remarks it if she does something outlandish. And she has become more and more so with each passing Season."

Yardley grunted.

"Did you spy on them?"

Yardley arched a haughty eyebrow. "I would not call having an eye for my sister's welfare spying. He is the first person I have seen her react to in such a way, and he appeared to be equally enchanted." He did not seem pleased by the revelation.

"Yet you do not want him anywhere near her." She folded her arms over her chest.

"How could you consider him to be worthy of Charlotte?"

"Cavenray says he is a reformed man." She countered.

"I am delighted for him. As long as he stays away from my sister."

"Benedict," Jolie warned.

"Even if I were to overlook his scandalous past, he is still at the mercy of the King, his current title belongs to his nephew, as does his estate and fortune. He has nothing to recommend him but a criminal record!"

"If our families support him, there is nothing about his situation that cannot be portrayed in a heroic light. Society loves a reformed rogue."

Yardley scowled and brushed back a lock of blond hair that had fallen across his handsome brow.

"Do you think she realizes it is him? Besides, Charlotte will return to Langborn and not venture out for months until there is a compelling reason for her to do so."

"She has already refused my offer of returning to Yardley with us," he agreed.

"So there will be little cause for them to associate. I am certain there is nothing for you to concern yourself over," Jolie said, careful not to allow any hint of her plan into her voice, as she drew her husband into her arms to distract him from his foul mood. "So you may go and lend your support, at the very least."

"Very well," he agreed reluctantly. "But only for you."

DAVID FIDGETED and paced as he waited in the antechamber to the King's Drawing Room. The Duke of Yardley, the Duke of Cavenray and his nephew, now Lord Dannon, were all having a private audience with the King on David's behalf. No matter the prestigious names speaking for him, he was still nervous and his palms were sweating like a schoolboy about to go before the headmaster. He had no idea what to say to the King if he even granted him an audience. The truth was, he *had* been a free-trader, smuggling goods illegally. He *had* killed people in self-defence, and he *had* kidnapped his nieces and nephew for their own safety. On the other hand, he had done some things to atone for his sins—but were they enough? He saw how Seamus, Catriona, Maili and Letty had become wonderful adults and felt a small spark of pride at his part in that. He had freed all of his slaves and felt pleased with the knowledge that he had done the right thing. But were those enough recompense for his youthful indiscretions?

He sat back down and put his head in his hands, ruffling his hair. What would he do next, if he were free? The title and estate in Westmorland really belonged to Seamus. He had always had an interest in horses and he had enough money to begin a respectable stud farm. Yardley owned one of the best in England and perhaps he would give him some advice. He still could not believe that Lady Charlotte's brother was here, speaking for him today. It did not mean he would condone David courting his sister—certainly not if he knew he had been with her on the terrace the night before. That was another matter entirely, especially when he himself agreed he was unworthy to wash her feet. Yet, that kiss...he shook his head. He had stolen it, knowing she was too innocent to know what she was saying. He must stop thinking of her!

What else was there left for him? He could always return to his plantation and rebuild the manor house. There was always America, where many people had chosen to begin a new life. It was all so daunting, but something inside him wanted to remain at home.

The large white and gold door opened and a liveried footman stepped out.

"His Majesty will see you now, sir."

David walked into the bright red room, ornately decorated with gilt and boasting large chandeliers. He bowed deeply to the King. He had seen him as the young Prince Regent but the years of dissipation had not been kind to him. He was very portly and struggled to breathe, but his eyes held intelligence. David waited for His Majesty to speak.

"I hope, should I ever find myself in a pinch, I would have such loyal men to speak on my behalf. 'Tis still hard to believe Brennan was the mastermind of the smuggling operation for all those years, beneath our noses. I am obliged to you for your part in stopping him. Have you anything to say for yourself?" he wheezed.

"Thank you, your Majesty. I will confess to being a rogue in my youth. I have learned the error of my ways and can promise to be a loyal citizen to the Crown now."

The King chuckled appreciatively, which brought on a fit of coughing. "Lord Dannon says he does not wish for the baronetcy and estate of Crossings to be taken from you. He says his hands are quite full with the Dannon holdings. Will you also refuse them?"

David did not know what to say. This was wholly unexpected.

"Astonishing, is it not? I have never seen such goodwill amongst men. Perhaps I should set you all amongst the Tories and put them in line." He chuckled at his wit.

David was speechless.

The King's face straightened. "However, I do think I could use your help in a little matter." He waved his corpulent hand. "Earn your pardon."

David's heart sank. Of course it could not come so easily.

"Since you have intimate knowledge of the free-traders, I thought to set you amongst the Rottingdean gang, to see if you can help disband them. They are becoming a demned nuisance. They killed some of my men and are raiding my ships."

It could also be a death warrant for him, David realized while the King had to pause to catch his breath. "Your Majesty, if I may, it is common knowledge that it was I who betrayed Brennan. No one would trust me within a mile of the coast, now."

The King wrinkled his brow, clearly not pleased with his plan being contradicted. The advisor, a nondescript gentleman in black, shifted uncomfortably.

"Then do not let them know who you are," King George said in a fit of petulance. "When the Rottingdean gang is brought down, you may have your pardon."

"Yes, your Majesty."

Seeming somewhat mollified that David had agreed to his plan, the King nodded and excused them with a wave of his hand as the servants swarmed in to attend His Majesty. David released a sigh of frustration. He could live without the title or estate. He only hoped His Majesty would be so accommodating if he failed to destroy this group.

"I am grateful for your efforts on my behalf," David said to the others once they were outside St. James's Palace and waiting for their mounts.

"I wish your pardon had not been conditional. Is what he asks possible?" his nephew asked as they mounted and made their way north on Albermarle Street toward Mayfair.

"I suppose if Brennan was brought down, then Captain Dunn can be. However, I had a great deal of help in making that successful."

"We will help however we can," Cavenray assured David, having been part of the group which had helped foil Lord Brennan. "I assume the gang operates out of the village with the same name?"

"His trails run near my Langborn estate, in fact," Yardley finally spoke.

He had said nothing up to this point, David had noticed, still wondering why he was there.

All of the men turned to look at Yardley with surprise.

"They have never been violent, or bothered my land or peoples, so I have not felt the need to pursue it," he explained.

"They must have done something else to have wrought the King's ire," Cavenray said.

"Do you have any idea where to start?" David's nephew, Seamus, asked.

"Lady Brennan and Letty will be arriving soon at Wyndham for her convalescence; you could join them there. It is not too far to Langborn," Lord Craig suggested.

"I do not want anyone to associate them with me. The only way to bring a gang down is from within—become one of them. I will need to live like them."

"Let us know how we may help. You saved our lives once," Seamus pleaded.

David shook his head. "I cannot risk your lives again. Captain Dunn is rumoured to be every bit as nasty as Brennan, and he has less to lose."

"It does not mean we cannot offer assistance," Cavenray suggested.

"There is a cabin on my property you may use, on one condition," Yardley interjected.

David and the others all turned to look at Yardley with astonishment.

"You stay away from my sister."

CHAPTER 3

In my new pique of independence, choosing to ride for the first time in heaven knows when, I could barely button my habit today. If that were not humiliating enough, I can scarcely feel my bottom and my every joint aches. It was, however, invigorating and I must resolve to renew daily exercise. I fear I am becoming my mother. But why, oh why, are biscuits so hard to resist?—1 Feb

*M*elancholy is a very real part of an English winter. Even in the south, there was cold, damp and a biting wind coming off the Channel. All the chimneys had plumes of smoke rising from them, indicating a day best kept inside. Why had she agreed to a weekly tea at Wyndham Court, the estate of Lord and Lady Easton and the Earls of Wyndham? Much as she adored them, she would like nothing more than to stay in bed the entire day.

Charlotte groaned out loud. When had she become such a sorry case? *Sometime after graduating from Miss Bell's finishing school, is when it began,* she thought. She could recall the sadness and loneliness she had felt those first few months at home, away from her friends. She had ceased to be herself then, burying her emotions in novels and biscuits. She had endured a short-lived come out, but when her brother's divorced wife returned, causing scandal, they had retreated to the country. Lady Olivia, her dearest friend, had still made a match with the younger Captain Harris that Season, while Charlotte had returned home to her eccentric mother—and had dabbled in ten spinster Seasons since then.

Burying her face in her pillow, she muffled her tears, trying not to opine over her one glimpse of what heaven might be like. She cursed David Douglas for giving her a taste. When she had thought herself content, he had stepped into her life—for not even an hour—and turned it upside down. Drat him for toying with her...but it had been magical! It was impossible to count the number of times she had relived the kiss or ached to find herself in his arms again.

Sitting upright with self-loathing, she threw a punch into her pillow sending downy feathers flying, thus causing the three cats atop her coverlet to pounce in a frenzy to capture them.

"No longer!"

What could she do? Her mother had tired of England, favouring the warm Mediterranean winters for her rheumatism. Charlotte was hardly in her dotage. She did not even feel eight-and-twenty! She was considered of far too high a station to become a companion or governess, yet Society restricted her from having other freedoms. If only she were a widow she could do as she pleased. Perhaps she should find one of her papa's old cronies and ask for his name...she shuddered. Such a plan could backfire. She had known of some men living well into their eighties and nineties and that would never do. Why could she not attract a real suitor? Of course, Yardley could arrange something, but could she bear a loveless marriage when she was surrounded by love matches?

Did that one night truly happen?

He had made her feel small and delicate—dainty even. Attractive.

Putting herself in front of the mirror, she looked what she was: a virginal spinster with little attraction and not worthy of attention. Her once blonde hair had faded into a dull golden hue; her eyes mirrored her brother's green—but they reflected her sadness. Her bosom overflowed from her dressing gown, a stark reminder her figure could be considered more suited to a scandalous profession. Should she accept her fate? But she was not like those other demure ladies sitting against the wall during balls. She did not like to gossip and titter and flutter her fan as though she enjoyed sitting with the octogenarians and wallflowers. Everyone else had proceeded with their lives. She was the last one alone.

Self-pity was such an ugly emotion. Well, why should she sit at home, feeling sorry for herself? How much damage could she really do to her reputation if she enjoyed herself a little? It was not as if she planned on opening a brothel or gaming hell or even racing a high-perch phaeton down St. James's. Maybe she would not attract anyone she wished to marry, but she could have a little fun and do something meaningful.

Lord and Lady Easton had orphanages and schools.

Lord and Lady Fairmont ran a veterans' home.

Lord and Lady Ashbury had a home for ruined women.

Her brother was active in the Lords with political reform.

Listing everyone else's causes only made her feel more worthless.

She shook her head and reached for the bell to summon her maid in order to dress for riding.

An hour later, she was mounted on her chestnut mare for the first time in years, heading towards Wyndham. Feeling emboldened by her decisions of the morning, she eschewed an escort and rode alone. Oh, no doubt there was a groom following discreetly behind her at the Duke's order, but she would allow herself to think she had freedom. Urging Minerva into a trot at the thought, she wondered what she should do to make herself happy.

As she cantered by the estate's cottages along the eastern border of Langborn, she caught sight of a tall man—a gentleman by his bearing, though a heavy beard masked his features. A flash of recognition crossed a familiar face a moment before she was too far past to look back or risk her safety doing so. Could it have been her mystery man come looking for her? A rush of elation shot through her before rational thought intruded. Why was there someone on her property? Could he perhaps be visiting the steward? She urged Minerva forward, vowing to take a break from novels and read some improving works. Her head was spinning fairy tales out of straw.

Charlotte knew something was wrong the moment she rode up the drive to Wyndham Court. The usual hustle and bustle of a large estate was absent and there was straw covering the drive in front of the house, the curtains were drawn and the knocker was off the front door. The old Earl must have finally succumbed to the lure of Heaven. Charlotte hesitated only a moment, but she did not turn and leave. Their families had been friends and neighbours her entire life and she would at least enquire if they were in need of anything before she left. She rode on to the stables and a groom took the reins from her. Once she arrived at the house, the long-time butler, Hendricks, opened the door before she reached it.

"Good day, Lady Charlotte."

"When did it happen, Hendricks?" she asked as she walked into the bright, marbled entrance hall.

"Just last evening. Lady Olivia came in time to say farewell," he said sadly as he moved to take her cloak.

"I will not stay and intrude, then. I was coming for our weekly tea. Could you please give Lady Wyndham a message when she is not indisposed?"

"Of course, my lady."

"Charlotte, is that you?" Elly, now Lady Wyndham, asked as she looked out from the drawing room, her usual merry self. "Do not stand on ceremony with us! You are as good as family. Do come in and meet our guests."

"If you are certain," Charlotte said hesitantly, and allowed Hendricks to take her hat and cloak before following Elly into the blue drawing room, which was warm and very welcome after the cold ride.

"Adam and Olivia are upstairs. He went peacefully, you know. He said he was ready to trade his old bones in," Elly said with a gentle smile. "He strictly forbade mourning, as well."

"That sounds like him." Charlotte smiled, though she had a lump in her throat. Anyone who knew the old Earl had instantly loved him.

"Lady Charlotte, may I introduce Lady Brennan and Miss Dickerson?"

Charlotte walked over to greet the strangers, who had been seated near the large stone fireplace. She thought Lady Brennan seemed familiar, but she did not recall anyone named Dickerson. It appeared that Lady Brennan could not use her legs, for she did not stand and was in a strange chair with wheels attached to it.

"It is a pleasure to meet you, Lady Charlotte. We have come at a horrific time, it seems. We were visiting Lady Wyndham to try some new treatments for my paralysis," Lady Brennan said, in answer to Charlotte's unspoken question.

"Yes, now they are insisting on leaving us, due to the Earl's death. Please help me convince them to stay! They mean to return all the way to Westmorland," Elly said, clearly exasperated although she sat down and poured Charlotte a cup of tea.

"Perhaps I may be of service? Would you feel more comfortable staying with me while things are settled here? I only live a few miles away and have more than enough room. My mother is travelling on the Continent, if you do not mind the quiet."

"I do not wish for you to leave at all," Elly insisted. "However, if it will keep you from leaving all together then I will encourage it."

Miss Dickerson looked to her mother, who gave a slight nod.

"We would be very much obliged to you, Lady Charlotte. Maili has mentioned that I should befriend you whilst here," Miss Dickerson spoke.

"I will be pleased to have you, especially if you are Maili's friend," she replied with a genuine smile. "It has been more lonely than I expected with Mama gone. Is there anything else I can do for you, Elly?"

"Nothing at all. I will send them in the carriage at their convenience. Olivia would want to see you before you go, though."

"Of course. I shall give her my condolences." Charlotte made her way up the stairs, wondering what she was getting herself into by offering to host Lady Brennan and her daughter. For Lord Brennan had been the one David Douglas had been involved with, had he not?

~

DAVID STOPPED short as he watched a lady pass by on a dark chestnut. Lady Charlotte was here? No wonder Yardley had made that command. He would have rethought Yardley's offer to stay here had he realized this is where his sister lived. Had Yardley known he was asking the impossible?

Brushing his hands along his scruffy beard, he did not think he had been recognized. On hindsight, he should have changed out of his gentleman's attire before arriving—not that it was of the first stare. Having changed, he ran his fingers under his scratchy wool shirt—the shirt he had never thought to wear again along with his 'Captain Deuce, the smuggler' persona. He had thought that mask buried along with Lord Brennan. Of all the things for the King to request of him, this never would have occurred to him! Exiling him back to Barbados, yes; paying an extortionate bribe, yes; but returning to free-trading? Never.

Pulling on his oldest boots, he sat in the small, upholstered chair in the cottage Yardley had provided for him to operate from. Having to be on Yardley's property, knowing his sister was there, was the devil's own punishment in and of itself. He must have seen them together that night at the ball and disapproved. Certainly, David had not intended to raise Yardley's ire, especially when he agreed with the Duke. He had no business being anywhere near Lady Charlotte. She had been on his mind entirely too much the past month and now, the possibility of seeing her often was going to make it impossible for him to get her out of his mind.

He was here as the supposed gamekeeper in said cottage, though there was not much game in these parts to be had other than the occasional wild boar and fox. Yardley had set him up nicely, however, for the larder was stocked and the place was cosy enough for a bachelor.

Having unpacked and donned his disguise, it was time to begin his mission here. He walked to the stables where he had left his stallion in the hands of most capable grooms. Even at his secondary properties, Yardley kept an impressive stock of cattle. Perhaps the Dowager and

Lady Charlotte were horsewomen. He would dearly enjoy watching more of Lady Charlotte handling a horse. What would he do if he came face to face with her again? It could happen, even if he took pains to avoid her. Would she recognize him in the light of day? By now, she probably knew who he was and had been warned away from him, even though he had tried to do so himself. It was very likely Yardley had guards escorting her about the property, with him in residence!

He had spent the past month trying to find out everything he could about Rottingdean's free-trading and he thought he had enough information to insinuate himself into the smuggling gang. It had been one thing, when he was a wild young buck, to become part of the operations locally where he was known. It was going to be another matter altogether to be trusted by a group that did not know him. He could never play the stupid, brawny fool and be mere manual labour for a gang. No, he would have to earn the leader's trust. He only wondered what the cost would be. He might have the King's authority, but it did not mean he would be protected from harm.

Entering the stables, he greeted each of the horses as he made his way to his own trusted mount, Gulliver, who was a horse befitting a giant such as he. He bridled and saddled the stallion himself as a beautiful chestnut mare nickered, trying to get his attention. She was a beauty to be sure, and perhaps, if all went well, Yardley would allow him to breed Gulliver with one of his stock when this was over. He would love to see the results of an Andalusian with an Arabian or other fine cattle—perhaps make a new breed and new name for himself. Lord Easton also had some of the best stables in England, and he hoped he would soon be able to visit them at Wyndham, along with his sister and Letty.

After he led his stallion out of the stable, he mounted and reluctantly headed toward the Black Horse Inn to begin his descent into his past life again.

The inn was much as he imagined it would be—like any other you would find along an English road. It had a low-hung ceiling inside, with dark wooden walls, and the odour of smoke, ale and sweaty men greeted his senses. David had come purposefully early in order to watch the usual crowd gather. There was a full moon and clear sky, so no smuggler worth his salt—or his neck—would be out working his trade that night with the Revenue about.

He removed his hat and gave a nod to the innkeeper as he chose a discreet table towards the back of the tap-room.

A lusty-looking wench approached him with a saucy smile. "You'll not want to be sitting there, sir. That's where Cap—some usual customers sit."

"Well, since I'm looking to become usual I'd best find my own table. Where do you suggest?" he asked, reminding himself to lose his Etonian accent.

"'Tother side, sir. Are ye new here, then?"

"Aye. Just in from the West Indies. I've taken the gamekeeper's post at Langborn House."

"Welcome to ye, then. I'm Gertie and if you're ever needing something more fulfillin', you know where to find me." She winked. "Will ye be wantin' some meat pie with yer ale?"

"Please. A pleasure to make your acquaintance, Gertie, I'm called Douglas." That was the name he had settled on. Captain Deuce would be known even here. He tried for the balance between interest and open invitation. She would be a source of information in the future.

"The pleasure will be all mine, I'm sure," she said with a saucy grin as she turned and walked towards the kitchen with an enticing sway of her hips.

The food was decent, and the ale good. David sat and watched the villagers slowly come in from their day's work. It was easy to spot the leader of the gang. Having been one, he knew all the signs. A man in charge had a certain aura about him and the other men were deferential, whether they realized it or not. Captain Dunn looked like a weather-beaten sailor, with leathered skin, grizzled hair and dark, beady eyes which looked very sharp.

As he suspected, there were whispers and not-so-subtle glances in David's direction, and Gertie was the one to supply the answers to their inquisitions.

David slowly drained his ale and wiped his mouth before rising to his feet and throwing some coins on the table. Putting his hat back on, he gave a small nod of acknowledgement to the leader and his men, then another smile and a wink to Gertie before he sauntered out of the door. His first order of business for the night had been accomplished.

CHAPTER 4

They say Hell hath no fury like a woman scorned, but I rather feel as though my brother will give Hell a run for its money when he hears of my plans...once he overcomes the shock of it. Why is it so difficult for men to give up control?—2 Feb

*E*ven the short journey from Wyndham was exhausting for Lady Brennan, so she was immediately shown to her room to rest. Fortunately, there were apartments on the ground floor to accommodate her wheeled chair, since the house was built partially into the hillside.

"This is one of the most beautiful places I have ever seen!" Miss Dickerson exclaimed as Charlotte led her into the drawing room. The room had an entire wall of floor to ceiling windows, overlooking the white chalk cliffs and English Channel on the Sussex coast. Even after living here for many years, Charlotte was not immune to its beauty.

"In the summer, I prefer to sit outdoors on the terrace, but if the fires are built up enough in here I can almost forget how cold and dreary it is outside." The rest of the room was charming and cosy, done in pale blues and creams with several comfortable sofas placed around the wall of windows for advantageous viewing.

"This is my first English winter since I was small, and I feel as though I shall never be warm again!" Miss Dickerson rubbed her arms as she spoke.

"Forgive my manners! I shall ring for tea. It will warm you."

"I did not mean to—" Miss Dickerson began to protest, but Charlotte just smiled and waved away her objections.

She walked over and rang the bell-pull before sitting down again. "I am unused to entertaining," Charlotte confessed. "Where have you been living all these years, then, if not in England?"

"An island named Barbados, on a sugar plantation. Do you live here all alone?" Miss Dickerson asked as she sat near the windows.

"My mother lives here with me, although she seems to have discovered an affection for wintering in the Mediterranean. I can scarce blame her since I too prefer a warmer climate. Perhaps I shall join her next time." Charlotte smiled.

"You would love the West Indies," the slight lady with intriguing blue-grey eyes and dark hair said. "It is always warm and the waters are incredible shades of blue and green," she added wistfully.

"I recently met someone else who had come from the West Indies," Charlotte recalled. She could still not quite make out the relationship to Sir David, though there must be one, and she dared not ask her at this early stage of their friendship, even though she searched for similarities between them.

"You choose to live apart from your brother?"

"My brother chooses to live apart from my mother, is more the truth of it," she answered dryly. "She prefers the milder climate, as do I. It is not to say we are at odds, but some families are more in peace with each other at a distance."

"I am becoming accustomed to a large family. I had never known family other than my uncle until recently. Now, it seems, I have aunts, uncles and cousins everywhere I turn!" she exclaimed.

"It can be a blessing and a curse!" Charlotte laughed.

"May I be so bold as to ask what you do with your time here? I saw little in the way of habitation for some distance," Miss Dickerson remarked.

"There is little to do," Charlotte agreed. "Our nearest neighbours are at Wyndham Court or at Loring Abbey. There is Brighton just west of here and not far from Wyndham is Newhaven. When we feel overly adventurous, we go to London or Brighton. Perhaps one day we may go there and see the King's Pavilion."

"I have no wish to become a burden. I am quite content to curl up with a book. I spend a good deal of time reading to Mama."

"Reading is what I do most here, but I have resolved this morning to do more with myself—take up a cause of some description."

"What would you like to do?"

"The problem is, I do not know. Every person of my acquaintance does something meaningful, like charity work, reform or politics. I have no head for politics, so I thought to see if I could join one of the ladies' movements in Town."

"I am certain they would be happy to have any help you could offer. There are always people in need. Even in Barbados it seemed there were always some poor beggar children."

"They are everywhere in the slums of London. I can scarcely bear to go to certain parts. Yardley donates large sums of money and works hard in the House of Lords to improve social reform, but it never seems enough. I just need to choose what causes to take up. I have decided to take my own house in Town this Season." Charlotte looked to see if she had scandalized her visitor, but there was no trace of reaction.

"I would dearly love to see London," Miss Dickerson said dreamily. "However, Mama is too embarrassed to be seen in Society. She says everyone will pity her and whisper behind her back."

"That much is very likely true. Gossip is rather synonymous with the *ton*."

"I also think she wishes to spare me."

Yes, there would be talk. Charlotte could hardly blame them.

"How did she lose the use of her legs? Was it due to illness? I am afraid I know very little of the story, myself." It was gauche of her even to ask, but Miss Dickerson did not seem to mind.

"Are you immune to gossip?" Miss Dickerson asked with surprise.

"Not at all! I had heard Lord Brennan was killed, and that he had been the mastermind of a smuggling ring."

"It was a horrid business," Miss Dickerson said, closing her eyes. "My uncle David had once worked for Brennan by smuggling. Uncle David fled to the West Indies with me as a child when he feared for my life and his. When we returned from Barbados, Lord Brennan blackmailed him into doing his nefarious work again. There is much more to the story, but when Uncle David confronted Lord Brennan on the beach near the Scotland border, my mother was shot and has not been able to use her legs since. She would not have lived if Lord Craig had not been there."

"What a horrible thing to be betrayed and shot by your own husband!"

"Indeed," Miss Dickerson agreed sadly. "I am glad to know my mother has been spared having to listen to the gossip. I hope to keep it that way."

"Yes, of course, Miss Dickerson. Perhaps you may visit Town with me sometime when your mother is visiting Lady Wyndham. It is not overly far and you need not leave your mother for long."

"I would enjoy that very much. I do not care what the gossips say about me. Please do call me Letty."

"I would be delighted, as long as you will call me Charlotte." They exchanged smiles.

Letty stood and walked to the window. "How far does this estate reach?"

"Quite some distance. It stretches to the sea on the south, and to the north and east farther than I care to ride. The western border meets with the Duke of Loring's estate on the northern half and the Wyndham estate to the south. There is a veterans' home and a medical training school for orderlies and nurses between those two estates."

"And this is only one of your brother's properties? I am still becoming acquainted with what being a duke means."

Charlotte nodded. "His country seat is near Birmingham. It makes Langborn seem minuscule."

"Our plantation in Barbados was large, as well, until a storm destroyed it."

"Is that why you returned?"

"Mostly, yes. The crops are still thriving on the land but the house has not been rebuilt. I think Uncle David longed to see England again and his family—what was left of it, anyway."

"Do you miss it?"

"It will always be home to me, but if we had not returned I would not have known my mother."

"You did not know your mother before?"

She shook her head. "Very little. I can see why you would be confused. My father was the old Duke of Cavenray and my mother is Lady Brennan. They eloped to Scotland, but her parents forced her to honour her arrangement to Lord Brennan. They were deeply in debt to him and he wanted Mama even though she was with child."

Surprise must have registered on Charlotte's face.

"If it offends you, mother and I can return home on the morrow," Letty added hastily.

"We cannot control the circumstances of our birth, Miss Dickerson. If your brother and mother choose to recognize you, who am I to say nay? Clearly you also have the support of Lord Wyndham, Lord Craig and the Duke of Cavenray. I am quite happy to have a friend near my own age. I am either in the company of young maidens or my nieces and nephews of late—every one of them horse mad. If you have any other topic of conversation, we will become fast friends. I am considered a spinster, and being the daughter and sister of a duke permits me some licence."

"Have you not wished to marry?"

"None who have offered, I am afraid. What of yourself, if I may be so bold? Would you like to partake in the Season, or find a husband?"

"I could not leave Mama. Even if I could, I imagine my birth would prevent most matches with those who matter in Society. Mama said the only matches I would be offered there would be of the scandalous sort."

"You are very beautiful. With your connections, your natural birth would not matter to most. Society is very fickle. Your brother is a powerful duke, and many would not gainsay him and risk his displeasure."

"I am not concerned about marriage. Having just found my family again, I am not ready to leave them yet."

"For myself, I plan to declare my independence this Season. I will find out exactly how much licence the *ton* will allow."

"And precisely how do you expect to do that, dear sister?" A deep, familiar voice boomed from behind.

"Benedict!" She jumped and whirled to face him.

"May I have a word?"

"WHAT THE DEVIL IS GOING ON?" Benedict demanded as they removed to the study, the one room Charlotte rarely entered when he was not in residence. It was a dark-panelled, masculine room with brown leather furniture and the complete opposite of her taste.

"I could ask the same of you!"

"You go first."

"The Earl of Wyndham died this morning. I found out when I arrived for my weekly tea with Elly. Lady Brennan and her daughter had just arrived from the north and felt as though they were intruding. They were about to leave."

"Intruding at Wyndham? That is preposterous!"

"We know that, but they are not well acquainted yet. Lord Craig had sent Lady Brennan there to the medical school to try some new treatments. Did you know she was paralysed from a pistol wound inflicted by her husband?"

"I had heard. I suppose you offered for them to stay here for the time being?"

"I did. And you would have done the same."

"Do not be so confident of my charity." It was going to complicate everything. How was he going to keep Douglas' presence from Charlotte with the man's family here?

"Now, you tell me why you are here."

"To visit my dearest sister, naturally." He arched one of his brows.

"Naturally."

"I hired a gamekeeper. I wanted to inform you and see how he is managing."

She eyed him with suspicion. "We have not had a gamekeeper this past decade. Do you mean to tell me you left Jolie and the children and rode down here just to tell me you hired a servant? You could have informed me by letter or sent a groom."

"Yes, but Jolie is in London with her *maman*."

"What is going on, Benedict?" She folded her arms over her chest, looking mulish.

"Why would I not come to see how you fare, knowing you are here alone? And why do you suddenly care how I manage my properties? What has happened to my demure sister?"

"I have never been demure," she protested. "Disinterested, perhaps. I have decided to become more independent. I wish to have my own house in Town this Season."

"No." His reply was deliberately curt.

"Benedict, you promised me."

"I promised you might do so when you are no longer of marriageable age."

She narrowed her gaze at him. "I am considered old enough to chaperone, Benedict."

"You still have much to offer, Sister."

"Please do not start this again." She nearly groaned; he could tell by her expression.

"You simply have not met the right man."

"I have been out for ten years, Benedict. *Ten*! I have met every eligible man in the kingdom."

"Two more years. When you reach your thirtieth birthday I will allow you your independence if you still wish it."

"Two more years? I must suffer two more years because you think I have not been trying hard enough to meet the right husband?" He could see she was trying to restrain her anger.

"I could arrange for you to meet some more eligible *partis* that do not go much into Society."

"No, thank you," she replied while biting on her lower lip.

Benedict held up a letter and waved it towards her. "Mother has married, Lottie. You cannot stay here alone."

"She…married?"

He held the letter out for her to read. He watched as she took and read aloud the epistle from their mother, full of the delights of the Mediterranean and its handsome men, encouraging Charlotte to join her and find one of her own.

She snorted and shook her head. "Unbelievable. She has left me."

Looking up, Benedict watched her with a commiserating gaze… except he could not truly understand how she felt.

"Take my offer, Lottie. It is not unreasonable for your elder brother to wish you well situated."

"I have been living here alone without any mishap, thank you."

"For a few weeks."

She glared at him sideways beneath her lashes. "I want it in writing."

"Now you question my word? I would call a man out for that!"

"You would not. After your history with duelling, you would do no such thing."

No, but he could not allow this madness. When had his little sister become so bold? "I will have my solicitor draw up the papers if you promise to try for two more seasons, including agreeing to meet some gentleman I arrange."

He watched her consider. "*Now* you add stipulations." She paused. "As long as the meetings are not obvious as such," she agreed grudgingly. "May I return to my company now?"

"Yes, of course. I need to pay my respects to Wyndham. I suspect Jolie will wish to as well. I will send a messenger for her."

He also wanted to have a word with Douglas. It would be more difficult to keep him away from Charlotte when Lady Brennan and Miss Dickerson were in residence. Perhaps it was a blessing he had arrived when he did. He would just have to stay and keep an eye on events, after he went and apologized to their guest for his rudeness. He did not appreciate surprises such as this—it was simply too much of a coincidence.

After jotting a quick note to summon Jolie and the children to Langborn, then greeting Miss Dickerson, as she was being styled, he bundled himself up for a ride to greet the new gamekeeper. He was distracted as he strolled to the stables, but not before noticing the stunning black Spanish horse gracing one of the stalls. He directed the groom to move the stallion to the last bay, not that Charlotte any longer bothered to exert herself by riding. If only he could convince her to apply herself just a mite, she would have multiple gentlemen clamouring at her feet. Instead, here she was, wasting away into a spinster. And now, Douglas was here...

Benedict should have known this would all explode in his face, leaving shrapnel in impossible places. He had extended the offer to Douglas on his familial connections and to please Jolie. Unfortunately, dear George would take the opportunity to use this for his own purposes. Benedict had seen no other way but to help Douglas gain his pardon. Oh, what a tangle this was going to be! Especially since his sister had got a bee in her bonnet about taking up a cause and becoming independent! Dash it all, she already was independent, but in an acceptable way. However, she was susceptible to Douglas and would it not be a coup for him to marry Charlotte and her dowry? Would it not be his toe in the door to social acceptance?

Benedict shook his head as he pulled up before the gamekeeper's cottage. Clearly, he had not thought this over properly before he agreed to such folly. He dismounted and tied Dido to a post before allowing her to graze.

What was done was done and they could only keep going and end this as soon as possible. He knocked on the door, not quite certain how he should address Douglas. He had not been cordial at their last meeting. Unused to questioning himself, he started at the vision before him—a figure looking exactly like a crusty old gamekeeper with a bushy beard, a flannel shirt and thick wool trousers.

"Douglas?" He could not mask the surprise in his voice.

"Your Grace, I did not expect to see you here. Come in." He stood back and held the door open.

Benedict held out his hand and gave Douglas a civil smile. "I did not recognize you."

Douglas looked taken aback at the gesture, but gripped his hand firmly. "Excellent. Hopefully no one else will, either. May I offer you some brandy?"

Benedict inclined his head.

"Please, have a seat and tell me what I can do for you."

Amused at this cordial reception, Benedict relaxed in one of two chairs by the fire. As Douglas handed him a drink, he continued to study the man with whom his sister was so taken. "I assume it is too early to have made progress?"

"I did as much research as possible in London on Captain Dunn and the gang, but it will take some time to insinuate myself into it. I have spent my evenings thus far at the Black Horse. The leader is aware of me and my new position here."

"Good. So it will not be taken amiss if we are seen together. Eventually, you will overhear something."

"Precisely. I already know enough to presume when their runs will be. I thought to observe a few and determine their style."

"Will you approach Captain Dunn?"

"It would be better to let him approach me. I need to know what I am dealing with before I stick my neck out there. I wish the King had been more specific about the nature of nuisance they are making. Smart smugglers know to stay away from the Crown, but Brennan was greedy and arrogant."

"An unfortunate combination. I can make some enquiries at Whitehall and with our Sovereign, if necessary."

Douglas narrowed his gaze. "Why are you helping me?"

Plain speaking; Benedict had to admire that. "I have a vested interest. My mother and sister live here, and if this operation has become a threat, then I need to eliminate the dangers."

Douglas made a little noise of agreement. "I will not refuse your help. Allowing me to use this cottage as a cover is a huge boon."

"Speaking of which, there is one more detail you should know. Lady Brennan and Miss Dickerson are now staying here."

"I beg your pardon?"

"The Earl of Wyndham passed away and they felt they were intruding."

Douglas cursed.

"My thoughts precisely. I have decided to remain here until this is resolved. We cannot be too careful. I had hoped to convince Charlotte to return to London with me, but she would not consider it now, with your family here."

"I cannot say I like any of them being here myself. My sister and Letty will return to Wyndham after the funeral?"

"That is my presumption."

"Do you not think your presence might inhibit operations?"

Benedict furrowed his brow while contemplating this possibility. "You could answer that better than I, but it is not unusual for me to visit one of my properties. We will need to warn the ladies, however."

"I had hoped to keep things quiet. The more people here, the more my presence will be noted."

"Where do your sister and niece believe you to be?"

The man ran his hand over his face and through his hair. "I told them part of the truth—that I had to work for my pardon and that I was looking for land to begin a stud farm. I had planned on visiting Wyndham to see his stables as well as visit my kin."

"I assume the lovely black stallion in the stables is yours? An Andalusian? I have not seen the like at Wyndham before."

"Aye, that's Gulliver. I hope to use him as a seed-horse when this ordeal is done."

"Perhaps we can make the most of our situation. I have a lovely snowy grey just outside. She is particular, but she was interested in your stallion in the stables."

"I am certain Gulliver would be most appreciative," Douglas chuckled.

"Excellent. I will see to it. After all, I will need something with which to occupy my time whilst here. It will be easier to explain his presence here—not that Charlotte rides any more," he muttered.

"May I send a note to Letty? I think it would be better if she knew I was here. I had told her I would visit them at Wyndham—"

"And now that is not possible." Benedict finished the sentence with a heavy sigh. "Yes, of course, but do you plan to explain the whole?"

"I think, perhaps, considering the changed circumstances, it would be better than her finding me by accident. If it happened at the wrong time, it could jeopardize the whole business. She can be trusted."

"I am less concerned now that I have seen you. I do not think anyone will recognize you as other than you are. You look every inch a gamekeeper. No one would think you the same Sir David from the Cavenray ball. If you wish to see Letty, I can help you arrange it."

Hopefully he would not live to regret it.

CHAPTER 5

Today I remembered why I have not galloped in years. It might be another decade before I can say the word again. I also discovered my guest is not as tranquil as I had credited her, and I could scarce keep up with her. It shall not happen again.—3 Feb

*H*ow is your mother faring this morning?" Charlotte asked as her guest joined her in the breakfast room. It was another bright space, papered in pale green and facing the gardens. Flowers from the hot house dotted the tables, bringing the feel of spring.

"Very well, thank you. I left her in the hands of her capable nurse, doing some exercises Lady Wyndham recommended."

"Please, do help yourself." Charlotte waved towards the buffet of food set out on the sideboard—bacon, eggs, kippers, fresh scones and more. She watched with envy as the little wisp of a thing piled her plate high.

"Very good. I am thankful she has something helpful to do while you are here."

"She insisted I enjoy my time with you, but you must not feel obligated to entertain me."

"I do not, I assure you," Charlotte said with an impish smile. "I was thinking to ride again today. Yesterday was my first long ride in some time and I had quite forgotten how invigorating the exercise is. I do, however, feel some muscles that I am certain I did not have before."

Letty laughed. "I would enjoy a ride very much. I have not been on a horse a great deal since I left the Indies."

"Then we shall not abuse ourselves as much as I did yesterday."

"Good morning," Benedict greeted them as he strolled into the room in his riding attire.

"Good morning. Have you already been in the saddle this morning?" Charlotte enquired.

"Of course," he answered with an insouciant air, beginning to fill his plate. He sat down as a footman began to pour his coffee.

"You seem more cheerful today. Does that mean Jolie will be joining us soon?"

His wistful smile was answer enough. How she longed for someone to miss her like that. "Yes, they are expected by tea-time." Lifting his knife and fork, he paused. "Miss Dickerson, I have a letter for you. I left it in the study, if you would join me there after breakfast?"

"Thank you, your Grace. Please do call me Letty. I am unused to the formalities."

Benedict inclined his head. "As long as you do not address me as 'your Grace' at every turn."

Letty smiled and Charlotte detected a resemblance to another smile she saw in her dreams. She sighed into her chocolate and tried to keep her attention on the present, wondering if Elly had sent over a note. It was too early for the post.

"Benedict, is there a mount you would recommend for Letty? We would like to ride this morning."

His eyebrows elevated in surprise. While it had been some time since she had evidenced any interest in anything other than her books, she had been brought up in the saddle like all the Stanton family. Ignoring his look, she continued, "I rode Minerva yesterday and she was in good form."

"Of course she is, or some grooms are out of a position. I have Dido here, and I am putting her to stud with an Andalusian while I am visiting. She is not in heat yet, so that can wait until later. How accomplished a rider are you, Letty?"

"I have been riding since the cradle."

"Then you can handle Dido. Mayhap a good ride will make her nicer to the stallion." He smiled and looked distant, as though lost in a memory. Then he started, placed his napkin on the plate and stood up. I will be in the study at your convenience, Letty."

"I will call for the horses to be ready in an hour," Charlotte said as they, too, finished the meal and rose to their feet.

Letty followed Benedict down the hall and Charlotte went to tell the butler to send to the stables for Minerva and Dido. As she walked back past the study, she overheard her brother and Letty still talking. Thinking nothing of it, she walked on to the stairs when she heard Letty ask, "Uncle David is here? At Langborn?"

Charlotte froze and strained to hear.

"He is my new gamekeeper. He wishes his presence to be kept quiet, however."

"Yes, of course," she heard Letty say sadly. "I just cannot fathom how it came to this. He is—or I thought he was—a wealthy landowner! Do you think the King will ever grant his pardon?"

"Who can say what George will do?"

"You think he is toying with him?"

"I cannot predict. He is very much used to having his way."

Letty sniffed as though struggling with tears. Charlotte felt conflicted as she eavesdropped, but she wanted to know more. Had the King refused to pardon Sir David? Then why was he free and working for Benedict? Was he wanted and hiding?

"Am I allowed to see him?" Letty asked.

"It is dangerous to acknowledge him openly. He is to be known simply as Douglas while he is here. I think it best to meet with him at the house as no one will suspect anything if he comes pretending to meet with the steward or owner. It will be harder to explain if you are seen going to the cottage."

43

"Yes, of course. I would never want to jeopardize his life! Was he very angry when he discovered Mama and I were here?"

"Not very, but he thought it best to warn you not to know him in public."

There was a quiet pause, and Charlotte knew she should leave before she was found listening.

"He does not deserve this, your Grace. He is a good man. Thank you for giving him a place."

"Let us hope it all works out in the end."

Before she could be caught, Charlotte hurried on up the stairs to change into her riding habit. Her mind raced with questions, the foremost being, was he her mystery man? If so, what could be done to help him?

An hour later, Charlotte and Letty were downstairs ready to ride. The grooms assisted them onto their mounts and Charlotte decided to take Letty on a tour of the estate. No one had warned her against seeing Sir David. Thank goodness she had overheard. What if she had, all unbeknownst, compromised his disguise? Yet why would Benedict keep it a secret from her? It made no sense.

"I thought I would take you on a tour of our property. That will be far enough for today."

"As long as we can view the cliffs," Letty said. "I miss the ocean dreadfully."

"I try to explain that to my brother every time he insists I move north. I enjoy London for a little while and then I must have the sea again."

"Your brother reminds me of mine. It is the ducal air about them, I suppose. It is all so foreign to me, having been brought up on a small island with mostly servant children for playmates."

"Yes, I suppose that would be different. Was there no gentry on your island?" she asked as they trotted along a path away from the stables.

"Oh, there were a few families, but Uncle David never felt particularly comfortable entertaining. There are not many ladies, and those there hunted him."

Charlotte could only imagine such a scene as she felts pangs of jealousy. "You were happy there, then?"

"I was. My uncle treated me as his own and I never wanted for anything." She smiled wistfully.

"He sounds like a good man. There is not much age difference, is there, if he is Lady Brennan's youngest brother?"

"He is less than ten years my senior."

"It must have been quite a responsibility to take you on so young."

"Indeed, but he never seemed to resent me."

They chatted on and Letty followed Charlotte's lead, not knowing they were taking the long route to the cliffs in order to pass nearby the gamekeeper's cottage.

"I hope this dreadful business will be over with soon."

Charlotte fell back to be next to her companion. "Do you refer to the business with Lord Brennan?"

"Yes. Apparently the King has not yet pardoned my uncle. I cannot understand it."

"I thought it was your uncle who uncovered Brennan's smuggling ring and brought him to justice?"

"It was."

Charlotte mulled these things over and could not decide her thoughts. She was forced to slow the horses as they came near a row of matching stone cottages at the point on the property where the grassy meadow they were riding through became forest. The nearest house belonged to the steward, and there were two empty cottages before they reached the farthest, which was the gamekeeper's. Charlotte and the Dowager passed very quiet lives and rarely entertained, so there was little need for the extra servants which went with a ducal residence. It did seem a shame that two perfectly good houses stood empty. They were charming, with their stone walls, thatched roofs and gardens surrounded by neat wooden fences. Perhaps she would discuss that further with Benedict. Smoke rose from the last chimney and Charlotte's heart began to race. She did not wish to be discovered stalking Sir David, even though she longed to see him. She turned the horse back towards the sea after pointing out the edge of the property to Letty.

"That road leads to Loring Abbey. The southernmost path would take you directly back to Wyndham."

"The path to Wyndham skirts the cliffs?"

"Yes."

"Race you to them!" Letty shouted as she turned Dido and urged her into a gallop.

Charlotte turned Minerva and the mare was pleased to chase after Dido. She would recognize the gleam in Letty's eye next time, however. It had been years since Charlotte had had a proper gallop or race, and it felt freeing. Or it would if she were not concerned about Letty misjudging the distance to the cliff's edge. Leaning over Minerva, she set about catching up with Dido—which was no small feat.

Years of riding served her very well when she would otherwise have been inclined to panic, for they were gaining on Dido at a spanking pace, as her brother would say. Unfortunately, Letty was heading straight for the edge of a ravine which she might not see in time to jump clear. Charlotte called out a warning to her companion and attempted to overtake her, but Minerva missed her footing, almost going down as her hind legs splayed. Charlotte had an instant to disengage her foot from the stirrup and the other from about the pommel before tumbling safely to the hard ground. She looked up to see Letty had traversed the ravine and was circling back to her.

"Charlotte! Are you hurt?" Letty asked as she pulled Dido up beside her and dismounted.

"Only some bruising. I think Minerva might have come up lame," she observed, looking at the mare. "I was terrified you would not see the ravine in time."

"I feel horrible! I know better than to race on unfamiliar territory!"

Letty helped Charlotte to her feet, then they walked over to where Minerva was standing, holding the injured leg away from the ground. She ran her hand down the leg, but could not determine the extent of the injury.

"Oh, you poor dear! Please let it be minor!" Letty said frantically.

"Do you think you can find your way back to the stables?" Charlotte asked.

"Yes."

"Go get Simmons and bring him back here. I will wait with Minerva."

Letty nodded and Charlotte boosted her up into the saddle. As Letty rode away, Charlotte turned to croon soothingly to the mare, praying she could be saved.

DAVID SWORE under his breath and dashed behind a large tree when he saw Letty and Lady Charlotte approach his cottage on horseback. Had Yardley not warned them?

He would have to rethink his plan. Endangering himself was one thing, but his niece and Lady Charlotte...

The object of his thoughts deftly manoeuvred her mare around and headed quickly in the other direction. Breathing a sigh of relief mixed with regret, he admired the way she sat the horse and commanded it with ease.

He shook his head with self-recrimination. He must stop yearning after what could never be. Had he been a few minutes earlier, he would have been caught by them as he returned to his cottage. Turning, he headed towards the cliffs to do his dirty work—work that labelled him a criminal and completely unfit for a duke's daughter.

Pulling his hat lower over his head, he thrust his hands into his overcoat and slouched, hoping to make himself even less recognizable. He deliberately forced himself to walk in a rough gait like that of a labourer as he climbed to the cliffs, looking for the pathway towards the beach. It was the same route the smugglers used on their way further inland to store their contraband.

It was a safe time to explore since most of the free-traders had daytime occupations. As gamekeeper, he was authorized to explore every inch of Yardley's land in the daylight. He made his way quickly down the rocky slope, having had years of experience along the coast of Westmorland—once innocently as a youth, and then in his reckless days as Captain Deuce.

He reached the cliff's edge, the wind whipping his coat against him as he held onto his hat. He was struck by the bright blue of the water at its shallowest, a similar contrast to the white beaches of Barbados. He had never before stood on the southernmost coast of England. The strength of the wind off the water and the sharp descent, should he misstep, gave him the desire to hurry this distasteful task along with due haste.

Pausing to glory in the majesty of the Creation, and take a moment to be thankful he was still free, he scanned the horizon and reminded himself no matter what the outcome, there was something greater than he. It was impossible to deny there was a greater power when he watched the force of the waves crashing against the rocks below, or the sun paint colours in the sky. Even being witness to the birth of a foal made him feel awe.

Looking westward from the easternmost point of the Langborn property, the cliffs sloped downward to a beach. There was no cover along the cliffs, just grassy downs, and he began to scout as he walked for signs of the trade. The drop to the beach was quite steep, he found, as his foot slipped and some of the earth gave way. There was not much beach to be had, especially some parts abutting the cliffs, making it a dangerous operation depending heavily on the tides.

He skirted the water's edge until there was an opening in the chalky rock. A pathway leading north was found right where Yardley had said it would be. With David's experience in the trade, he began looking for nearby caves or tunnels. There would have to be some entry point to make it a long-standing, reliable smuggling route to London.

He began to run his hands along the cliff face until he found what he was searching for—rocks, greenery—anything to disguise a cave for what it was. Looking around to make certain he was unobserved, he pulled back on the long tussocks of grass hanging down that were hiding a tunnel entrance. Beyond the initial entrance, which could be dismissed as a cave, a well-formed passage met his eyes, high enough for even he to walk through without stooping. He pulled a small lantern from underneath his overcoat and lit it with a flint.

He began to pace off his steps as he made his way upward through the opening in the earth. It was quite some distance before he met choices, and the damp, musty coolness pervaded his senses the further along he went. The fork to the right appeared as though it went back to Yardley's estate. He would investigate that one later. However, the other two pathways looked to have greater usage. He followed the one he judged to be in the direction of the village, and continued pacing his steps so he could retrace them later. By the time he climbed a flight of stairs and met with a door, he was fairly confident he was at the Black Horse Inn. He took out a small journal and made notes before retracing his route back to the central lane at the fork. Judging by the amount of oil left in his lantern, he thought he could follow one more route, though he could continue in darkness if needs must.

The second path appeared to end at a crypt. Could it be the village church? There was no sign of recent activity, no evidence of any storage taking place. That would mean Dunn either had a very efficient system to move their goods quickly, or they did small loads they could manage in one night.

The bright sun accosted his eyes as he came out of the cliff side. He looked around him as carefully as he could and hoped he was still unseen. Once he was clear of the tunnel, he began to ponder. It would be unsurprising for the local alehouse to assist in the free trade. After all, once the innkeeper had the goods, he was free to sell them. Nevertheless, the path to what he presumed was the crypt also appeared well used, and that could indicate compliance by the vicar—or at least him feigning ignorance. It had been known to happen and nothing, at this point in his illustrious career, would surprise him.

As he began to re-climb the path against the wind, he stopped short when he noticed a horse and a lady up before him. Lady Charlotte... alone, with no Letty in sight.

His first instinct was to run. Was she injured? If he stood there gawking long enough she would discover him anyway. Would she recognize him? Would Yardley seriously expect him to stay away from her if she was hurt? The question settled it for him and he climbed quickly to see if she needed help.

CHAPTER 6

How invigorating it is to be an independent woman. I can say and do as I please. Well, so far as I have been able to test my new-found character on my new friend, Letty. She is everything I have ever dreamed of being—dainty and delightful in a tactfully petite package. The complete opposite of myself. I want to hate her, but she is simply too perfect.—4 Feb

*M*inerva was growing more agitated and time seemed to slow. Charlotte considered; she could probably walk her mare back to the stables, but she was terrified to do her more harm. What if she caused more damage and the horse had to be put down? She stroked the dark chestnut neck soothingly and crooned reassurances, but it felt like she had been waiting forever in the whipping wind. What was taking them so long? Had Letty lost her way?

"Horse gone lame, my lady?"

Charlotte jumped and turned toward the deep voice behind her. "Oh! You startled me!"

"Beg pardon, miss. I was returning to my cottage when I noticed you here. I have a bit of experience with blood cattle, if you need help."

Charlotte eyed the stranger. He looked like a ruffian but spoke almost like a gentleman. His eyes were downcast beneath his hat, and his bushy beard obscured his face.

"Who are you?"

"My name's Douglas. I am the new gamekeeper, my lady." He gave a slight doff of his hat but kept his eyes averted.

The new gamekeeper? Good heavens! Charlotte's pulse began to beat frantically and a lump lodged in her throat. "I would appreciate your assistance," she croaked. "My companion went to fetch the head groom."

Sir David was already soothing Minerva by speaking in silky tones, and she was allowing him to examine her hock. It allowed Charlotte a moment to compose herself. She was not supposed to recognize the man, and perhaps she would not have if she had not eavesdropped. It was the first time she had seen him by day, and he was hiding himself. As she tried to discreetly take a closer look, he turned his back to her. Charlotte frowned.

Douglas began to walk Minerva slowly in the direction of the stables, watching her gait as she moved. The mare limped a little at first but began to move better as she went.

"Do you think it serious?" Charlotte dared to ask, refusing to be ignored.

"I think it merely a strain. She should come about with some rest. It will be some time before she can be ridden, though."

"Of course," she said, the disappointment evident in her voice— even to her own ears.

"I have heard the Wyndham stables are extensive. Mayhap the Duke can borrow another mount for you in the meantime."

"I am certain Yardley will accommodate me. I was rediscovering the delights of daily exercise, and perhaps over-exerted her." Charlotte blushed at her words. Never would she have been so forward with an unknown servant. She wanted to tell him she knew, but how would he react?

"No sense blaming yourself, my lady," he muttered.

Charlotte wanted to scream. He refused to look at her and was treating her deferentially, as though he did not know her, as though he had not kissed the wits from her the last time she saw him. And now she was to pretend she knew him not at all, even when alone? It was not to be borne!

"Sir David." There was no one else around to hear them, even if they could see.

She sensed him stiffen.

"Look at me and deny it." The command in her voice surprised even her.

Stepping forward and lifting her chin to look into his eyes, she was unprepared for the ice-grey stare that met hers. Her pulse began an erratic hammering, and breathing became difficult. They were standing so close she could feel his breath on her face. His eyes fell to her lips and she sucked in a gasp. Minerva nickered her jealousy and nudged them.

"You are mistaken, my lady." He turned away and began walking Minerva again.

"Impossible," she called after him. He kept walking purposefully and she felt the urge to stamp her foot. What did she hope to accomplish by pressing the point? Clearly he did not wish to renew their acquaintance, and it hurt. She followed behind, losing confidence by the moment. Perhaps he did not like what he saw by the light of day.

When they reached the steward's cottage, the path to the house separated from the path to the stables.

"We should part here. I will look after the mare. I cannot be seen near you."

Charlotte nodded, stifling the urge to sob. "I understand," she squeaked, though she did not—not at all.

He dropped the reins and pulled her behind a tree. His hands felt like a brand searing through her riding habit. She could recall those hands holding her before…

"This will not do, my lady. That night…was a mistake. As you can see, our stations are oceans apart. I need this position and if I am seen dallying with my betters I will lose more than my place."

"Why must everyone try to shelter me from the truth as though I cannot comprehend it? I know there is something afoot—yet you would rather lie to my face." Bold speaking, indeed. She could not believe she had just said such a thing.

He sighed deeply and searched her eyes. "I would like nothing better than to tell you this is a farce and that I could restore my good name and be worthy of you, Lady Charlotte. Sadly, that can never happen. The King did not pardon me, and I must work to earn it. As you see, this is not a game. I must remain Douglas the gamekeeper, and you must not acknowledge me other than you would another servant. It could mean life or death to me."

How could she convince him she was trustworthy?

He must have read her thoughts. "Forget that night ever happened."

"How can you ask such a thing of me?" Her eyes scanned his, begging for understanding.

He looked away and sighed deeply.

"I know about your past transgressions, Sir David. That is what they are—the past."

"Do not do this, my lady," he commanded in a low voice. "You are making this harder than it needs to be."

She shook her head as tears filled her eyes.

"Just look at me! We cannot be together. There is no imaginable way that this will have a good outcome, so walk away and forget about me." He turned and took Minerva's reins.

"I am afraid I cannot," she whispered to his back as she slowly followed.

They saw Letty and Simmons approaching in a cart, as if preparing for the worst. Letty tried to look aloof, but Charlotte saw the covert glance she cast her uncle's way. Charlotte noticed the quick look of affection that passed between the two. Without so much as a nod of the head, he turned and walked away from her to speak with Simmons. He might as well have cut her heart out and stamped upon it, for it was refusing to beat, causing painful constrictions in her chest.

"Charlotte?" Letty asked. "Is something wrong? They will take good care of Minerva."

Good gracious, Letty thought she was upset about the horse. She nodded distractedly, unable to speak without blurting out something unconscionable. Letty continued chatting amiably, and Charlotte used her years of polite breeding to muddle through the walk back to the house. When they arrived, the house was at sixes and sevens with the arrival of the Duchess of Yardley and the children.

"Charlotte! There you are! Rosie was looking for you."

"I will be certain to go to the nursery next," Charlotte said with a smile, thinking of her youngest niece.

"She is taking her nap now. Nurse can bring her down after tea."

"Benedict did not tell me you were bringing the children."

"We did not know how long we would be here." She smiled at the guests. "And we cannot abide being so far from them."

"Yes, of course. Are you acquainted with Lady Brennan's daughter, Miss Dickerson?"

"I have not had the pleasure." Jolie smiled again.

"Your Grace, the Duchess of Yardley, may I present Miss Letitia Dickerson?"

Letty curtseyed deeply.

"A pleasure to meet you, Miss Dickerson."

"Please call me Letty." She also smiled warmly.

"Shall we have tea?" Jolie asked rhetorically as she pulled on the rope to summon the tray.

"How was your ride, ladies?" Lady Brennan asked from where she sat by the fire. "Come closer and warm yourselves."

"It is incredibly beautiful here, Mama. You will have to allow me to take you to the cliffs, if we have a warm day."

"That would be lovely."

"Letty rode Dido today," Charlotte remarked as she chafed her hands in front of the flames.

"What did you think of her?" Jolie asked as the butler set a large silver tray of tea, sandwiches and delicacies before her. "She is Yardley's favourite mare."

"I can see why. She led me a merry dance up on the cliffs. So much so that I am afraid Minerva was injured chasing after us," Letty replied.

"Oh dear, I hope she will be all right," Lady Brennan said with a frown. Jolie waited for further explanation.

"It was my fault. I did not think to warn her of the ravine. I was attempting to catch her, but Dido took it beautifully, of course," Charlotte added.

"And Minerva?" Jolie enquired.

"The gamekeeper happened upon us while Letty had gone for help. He thinks it only a strained hock."

Three sets of eyes watched her closely. Without missing a beat, she decided to play devilish. "He certainly looks familiar."

"All gamekeepers have the same look about them," Jolie said with a dismissive wave of her hand.

"If you say so," Charlotte replied in her best aloof voice, while scheming about how to force them to confide in her.

DAVID SEETHED with frustration as he walked back to the stables with Simmons and Minerva. He decided he would saddle Gulliver and go for a ride to clear his head. However, when he reached the stallion's stall, he was not there.

"The Duke has him out in the paddock with Dido, sir," one of the stable boys said when he saw David. He gave a nod of thanks to the boy before slamming his fist against the stall partition.

"Could this day get any worse?" he muttered to himself.

He had hoped to clear his head before speaking to Yardley. He was going to have to tell him of his conversation with Lady Charlotte. It was better the Duke should hear it from him than someone else. Steeling himself for a confrontation, he willed his temper to calm. For a few moments he stood outside the railed paddock, watching Gulliver court Dido. He had to chuckle. She was a spirited one, all right. Despite her long ride, she was out there prancing and playing coy with his stallion. He frowned. How he wished he could play the courtship dance with Lady Charlotte!

"You are a poor sop to be jealous of your horse," he chided himself.

He had nearly come undone watching Charlotte's face at his rejection. She deserved so much more than he could give her.

"Douglas," Yardley greeted him as he noticed his presence and walked toward him.

"Your Grace."

They watched the two horses as they performed the mating game, leading the grooms on a merry dance, Gulliver watching Dido with interest. The familiar smells, sights and sounds of horses, stables and paddocks surrounded David and suppressed the anger rising within. This is what he should be doing instead of masquerading as a smuggler.

"Dido is as particular as a diamond of the first stare being fired off in London," Yardley chuckled.

He grunted agreement with the analogy. "She will not be able to resist Gulliver for long."

"No. She is behaving in a far more cordial fashion towards him then she did my Hector."

"Mm." David replied distractedly.

"I cannot wait to see their offspring." Yardley was still chattering away about horses. "Is something amiss, Douglas? You seem preoccupied."

"Beg pardon. It is your sister." He sighed.

Yardley's gaze narrowed and his amiability was gone in a flash.

"I was out scouting for tunnels this morning, along the beach. When I came back over the cliff, I found your sister alone with her horse gone lame."

Quickly on alert, Yardley began to head for the gate.

"Everything is taken care of, your Grace. 'Twas only a strained hock and Minerva is back in the stables. Lady Charlotte seemed unharmed, but I thought you should know she recognized me."

Yardley let go a string of oaths.

"I apologize for breaking my word, but I could not leave her there until I knew she was unharmed."

"No, of course not. I appreciate your assistance. What did she say to you?"

"She was quite put out when I tried to insist she was mistaken, and told her it would not do for her to be seen being friendly with the lower orders."

"And she accepted that?" Yardley asked, wide-eyed.

"She seemed to, but there was a look in her eye I could not be assured of. Do you think we should tell her the whole?"

"Are you mad? At least my mother is not here, but I have a feeling there might be a good deal of meddling going on should we do such a thing."

David frowned.

"Just so. Leave Charlotte to me. I will make certain she does not interfere."

David did not want her to interfere—he could not bear the distraction—but he felt she should be told more. He had a feeling she would be more complacent if her feathers had not been ruffled—and ruffled they were, in a most alluring fashion.

"Did you discover the tunnels?" Yardley asked, pulling him out of his distracting visions of Lady Charlotte in a taking.

"Oh, aye. The entrance was where you suspected. I followed it back to a fork with three pathways."

"Three? Is that unusual?"

"Not particularly. I paced the first off to where I suspect is the Black Horse. The second ended at a crypt, and the third veered off to Langborn."

Yardley's brows lifted in surprise.

"Any idea where it leads?"

"None, but Jeffries, our butler, was brought up at Langborn. He will know."

David nodded. "I expect a run tonight, so I plan to reconnoitre."

"How can I help?"

"Might you discover where the tunnel leads? It looked less used than the others, so it may well be dormant."

"And if it is not?"

"Then it gives me another foot in the door."

CHAPTER 7

I suppose, when it is time to change, it is appropriate to mark the occasion with something physical. Who needs hair, anyway? It will grow back, will it not? Now I want to do more, but how?—5 Feb

Charlotte and Jolie sat in the carriage on their return from Wyndham. It was already past dark with only the moon to light their way. Snuggled beneath a warm blanket, with hot bricks at her feet, she did not envy the postilions braving the cold night. Still reeling from Sir David's earlier rejection, followed by the wake for the Earl of Wyndham, Charlotte was near desolate and struggling to master it. The men left to attend the funeral and interment, but the ladies and their 'delicate sensibilities' stayed behind—except Elly, of course. She still thumbed her nose, though regally, at Society and their view of ladies as being porcelain dolls.

Charlotte envied Elly for being able to be herself. Would Charlotte ever have that freedom? Death was always a cause for reflection, and the Earl's was no exception. It was his time, of course, and he had lived much longer than ever expected, but it still gave her pause. Coupled with Sir David's refusal to so much as acknowledge her...she felt like doing something outrageous. Yet, duty had been so deeply ingrained in her upbringing that she struggled with how far she would go. But she must do *something*.

Would independence be enough? She also wanted to be herself—but how? Nothing so scandalous as to shame her family, but could she not do something for herself for once, rather than what Society expected? Society—what a monstrous weight upon her shoulders, to be sure.

Her beautiful sister-in-law, Jolie, was also a person Charlotte admired. Being a duchess, Jolie also enjoyed rather more than normal lenience with her eccentricities.

Besides uncommon beauty, both Elly and Jolie enjoyed doting husbands. Deep in thought, Charlotte wondered if there was any way at all for her to enjoy life as they did.

"What are you thinking, dear Charlotte?" her sister-in-law asked from the opposite seat.

"About the future," she said vaguely.

"Yes, death has the tendency to make us reflect. Have you come to any conclusions?"

Charlotte sighed loudly. It was one thing to think things, but revealing her innermost source of inadequacy was another. Although, if anything had been on her mind lately, it was that she had nothing to lose.

"I want to learn to be myself," she said quietly.

Jolie stared at her thoughtfully, as though trying to read her mind. Charlotte could see her face by the light of the moon as they jostled along.

"And who do you think yourself to be? Who is the Charlotte inside you?"

How could she explain? "That is a difficult question to answer—to put into words."

"You need not answer all at once. Your brother and I will help however we may. You do know he only wants what is best for you?"

"Of course. However, he often has his mind made up beforehand on what that should be."

Jolie chuckled. Even her laughs were beautiful.

"I have accepted that I will be independent," Charlotte paused.

Jolie kept quiet, allowing her time to organize her thoughts. The sounds of the horses' hooves clopping along the cliff path, with the waves hitting against the rocks, soothed her and she continued.

"I feel I need a change. I have been hiding for so long I think I have ceased caring about life happening around me, preferring to escape into a good story."

"And now that has changed?"

"I want to do something bold, Jolie. I feel life is passing me by."

"What do you wish to do? What do you dream about when you are alone?" she asked, her voice filled with curiosity.

"Therein lies the problem. I do not know. I do not allow myself to dream."

"*Sacre bleu!*" Jolie whispered and Charlotte saw her shaking her head. "Your first Season I saw a glimpse of boldness. What happened? Was it cut short because of the situation with Lillian?"

Charlotte had thought Jolie unaware of how much that had affected her. Having been hesitant to have a Season to begin with, she had mustered up the courage to change her appearance and face the fashionable world. Nothing had then come of it because they had had to remove to the country quickly to avoid scandal after Benedict's first wife had reappeared.

"Would you allow me to help you? Make it up to you?"

"There is nothing to make up, I am afraid. A monkey in silk is a monkey no less. Or should I say a pig?"

"Oh, my dear. I could not disagree more. You hide yourself underneath drab clothes and mob caps. Forgive my plain speaking, but I think you have been afraid to show the world the real you. Something or someone has awakened your spirit and I think you should allow it to show."

Charlotte choked on a denial, except Jolie had hit upon the truth. Transformation was doubtful; however, what had she to lose? The worst that could happen was her pride would be injured and she remain at Langborn until she was wrinkled and grey.

"What do you propose?"

"Do you trust me?"

"How could I not? You set the fashion for the *ton*."

"Very well, I suggest you continue riding every day. Exercise improves your colour and health... and when your health improves, you glow on the outside."

Charlotte felt her face warm inside the carriage. She knew she looked unkempt, and Jolie was being ever so tactful about it. "I do feel better since taking up riding again." Her habit also fit better. Her own mother never exerted herself to restrict anything.

The carriage turned into the gates of Langborn. Having alighted, Jolie led Charlotte to her own apartments.

Jolie's maid, Jenkins, was rumoured to be the genius behind the Duchess' ever impeccable appearance, and she quickly requested her aid.

"Jenkins, I need your assistance in bringing Lady Charlotte *à la mode*." Jolie led Charlotte to her dressing table and seated her before the looking glass.

"Yes, your Grace," the maid said with remarkable calm, acting as though such a pronouncement was a daily occurrence. Both ladies stood behind her, examining, as though she were a piece of art they were uncertain about.

"I think short hair," Jenkins pronounced after a few minutes' interval, "and a new wardrobe with lower waists. No more of those sack dresses for you, my lady."

"We tried this once before and it made little difference," Charlotte argued. She had become rather fond of hiding her curves under shapeless gowns.

"Change takes courage, dearest," Jolie reminded her with a kind smile. "Besides, we are not changing who you are on the inside, only allowing your true self to shine."

Jenkins began reaching for a pair of scissors. "Wait!" Charlotte cried. "Perhaps we should choose the wardrobe first? I need time to become accustomed to this."

"No. I think that would be a bad idea. You will change your mind." Jolie protested.

The maid began pulling pins from Charlotte's hair, causing the heavy locks to unleash several feet down her back.

"My lady, if you cut your hair to here..." She indicated a place between Charlotte's shoulder and ears. "...then you will have beautiful curls and accentuate the shape of your face."

Charlotte frowned doubtfully.

"If you do not approve, it will still be long enough to pin up."

Charlotte could not remember the last time she had cut her hair. "I am not altogether certain I can pull this off, but it will eventually grow back. Go on, then."

"There is the spirit." Jolie beamed with approval. "Whenever I feel in need of a change, I always begin with my hair."

Charlotte closed her eyes as the ominous sound of the shears slicing hair rang in her ears. It was time to write her own story, and this was the beginning.

LYING FLAT ON HIS STOMACH, in a most undignified fashion, David waited for the tell-tale signs of the trade. There were no good hiding spots anywhere near the cave, so he had had to resort to the cliff's edge above the beach, his only shelter the tall grass. It was a perfect evening, with only the barest sliver of a moon and thick cloud cover. He much preferred the conditions of Westmorland, with multiple caves and trees for cover.

He had seen the men congregate at the opening some time ago, so he knew he had been correct about there being a run tonight. When the waves were about to lure him to sleep, he finally saw the flash of light indicating the arrival of the goods. The crew was efficient as he watched them roll out of the caves like ants marching toward a picnic. It was a far larger crew than he expected as he watched man after man gather the loot and begin making their way on shore. Surprisingly, half of the men began to take the pathway towards town through the Saltdean Gap—a very bold proposition in light of the lack of conceal-ment! Most of the men had a barrel under each arm as well! He watched as a fine horseman rode back and forth across the cliffs in the distance—most likely a lookout—and perhaps their mysterious leader. It was impossible to identify them from this distance on a dark horse, especially with his face hidden by the brim of his hat and upturned collar.

David muttered to himself. He still could not believe he was having to do this distasteful mission. He was paying for the sins of his youth indeed!

Near frozen from the biting wind and from being still so long, he was about to move when he saw the Revenue Officer. He had but an instant to make a decision, so he let out the whistle of alarm familiar to anyone in the trade.

David could only see one officer, but who knew where else they could be hiding? The smugglers heeded his warning and began to scatter. David may not be in the trade any longer, but he did not like to see anyone in the hangman's noose, not when the main reason they were doing this was to feed their families. No sane man would be out in the winter's cold otherwise.

He heard shouting and he stood, not fearing for his discovery any longer. He shuffled down closer to the gap, in order to see what was taking place.

"Howard! I know it is you!" Shouting to the dark sky, the officer demanded, "Show your face!"

David heard a rumble of laughter, followed by the sounds of a horse galloping away.

The officer cursed loudly and then made his way down the gap. By this time, the smugglers had escaped.

David continued watching as the lone officer held a pistol to the mouth of the cave. David should escape too, but never before had he been on the other side of an operation.

The poor beggar did not stand a chance, David reflected. If he was not brave enough to enter the cave, he had already lost his prize for the night.

Returning to where Gulliver was tethered, David mounted and made his way to the parish church. It was the farthest tunnel, but he had a suspicion that was where the bulk of the goods would be stored. He had no doubt the barrels taken directly up the road went to the Black Horse, where they would be safe once inside.

What did one officer hope to accomplish alone? If the King was so keen on bringing this gang down, why did he not provide more help here? What exactly did he expect David to do by himself? He arrived first, being above ground and on horseback, and hid behind one of the large stone graves on the periphery. The church was in the centre of the town, and did not offer many spots for concealment. He watched and listened as he confirmed his earlier suspicions. The men poured from the crypt and loaded several of the tombs with barrels and trunks of smuggled goods. While there was nothing unusual in this, one aspect of the scene was. The most surprising part of the whole operation was the sight of the vicar arriving and then directing proceedings, not Captain Dunn.

David frowned. This was the first whiff he'd had of the local vicar being involved. It was not uncommon for men of the cloth to take part in the free trade—many of them were vastly underpaid and brought up to a gentleman's way of life, liking their brandy as well as the next man. However, this must be a new development and perhaps the key to discovering what was behind the King's interest in the Rottingdean gang.

David waited for several minutes past the last noise he heard, to be certain he was alone. He then went methodically to each of the storage sites and inspected the illegal cargo. It really was shameful how easy it had been for him to trace this gang so far. Was it because of his own experiences or could the Revenue Officers really be so daft? To be fair, they did have rules about having proof and witnesses, but it just seemed so obvious. Or could there be more to this operation than he had yet seen? There must be.

Forcing open one of the heavy stone lids and sliding it aside, he found nothing unexpected. Lace, tea... in another he found salt, and some already bottled brandy—perhaps the most significant item. There were no markings to identify from where it had originated.

Carefully replacing the heavy stone lid, he then walked back to where Gulliver was patiently waiting for him. It was quite late by this time, and he almost expected to see the sun peeking over the horizon. As he placed one boot in the stirrup, Gulliver's ears flew back on alert. David paused and listened. It was likely nothing more than an owl, but he could not risk making himself known yet. There would be no thought in the smugglers' minds but to kill him before asking questions. Who would it be at this hour? Normally, the goods would be stored for a day or two before being picked up and transported on to London and the illicit trade routes. Once the goods reached that far they were virtually untraceable.

It was still pitch black and David heard the cart before he saw it. He squinted to make out what was before him, but it was a donkey cart and an innocuous-looking old gentleman. He proceeded to load the back of the cart from goods left under a table tomb, and then left as quietly as he had come.

After mounting Gulliver and turning him in the direction of Langborn, David pondered what he had learned and what his next move should be. If there was someone else directing something nefarious under the Crown's nose, he would only find it through Captain Dunn or perhaps the vicar.

"Ho there!"

David looked up to find Yardley riding an Arabian mare back to the stables.

"Your Grace. What are you doing out this late?"

"Attending Wyndham's funeral. What do you think of this mare I brought back for Charlotte?"

"She is a beauty, to be sure." He dismounted and stroked the sleek bay nose.

"Were you able to observe anything this evening?" Yardley asked as they handed the horses to a sleepy-looking groom. David waited to answer until they had walked away from the stables.

"The usual sort of activity. Most of the goods are stored in graves at the parish church." David reached into his greatcoat and pulled out a bottle of brandy he had taken.

"What have you there?"

"Research," he replied, giving the Duke a devilish grin.

"Then I suppose you had better come in and let us have a sample... on behalf of the Crown, of course," he added dryly, leading the way to the front door and letting them both in. David assumed the staff had been told not to wait up.

"With our expertise, perhaps we can narrow down its source. I suppose it is our duty, after all," David parried, enjoying Yardley's company with chagrin. He had not wanted to like the man, and were it not for Lady Charlotte...he did not blame the man for thinking him inadequate to kiss the ground she walked on. So why was he being so amicable?

David looked over the bottle for markings as Yardley went to a cupboard for tumblers.

"The brandy comes clear and undiluted in casks," David explained. "For the brandy to already be diluted to drinkable strength, and in bottles, means the churchyard is the site of an extensive operation. I witnessed the vicar directing the storage of goods..."

"Reverend Howard?" Yardley asked as he poured the caramel-coloured liquid into the glasses.

"I did not hear his name, but it was the first I had heard of anyone giving orders other than Dunn."

Yardley took a sip, looking contemplative.

"Is Howard from a well-connected family?"

"I could not say at the moment. I own his living, of course. I believe he has been here less than two years—a recommendation from some connection or other."

David nodded absently, taking his own sip.

"Do you think there is another peer involved, like Brennan?"

"I do not know what to think at the moment. It is still too early for me to show my hand, and I have not seen anything to warrant such interest from the palace. Anything is possible."

"This is high-quality brandy," Yardley remarked as he looked into the remnants of his glass.

"It certainly warms your insides after a cold night." David stood to leave.

"I will have Howard looked into and let you know."

"In the meantime, it looks like I will be going to church," David said ruefully, offering a sardonic salute to the Duke.

It was late, and David wanted nothing more than his warm bed. He bade Yardley farewell and walked out of the library and straight into Lady Charlotte.

CHAPTER 8

Never before had I truly appreciated the servants' network of gossip—never before had it been so pertinent. It seems my mystery man has caused speculation below stairs and the maids have all taken to wagering on which one of them he will choose! If I have to listen to Chapman drone on about his brawn or his fine eyes one more minute, I might lose my chocolate all over her dress. Now, if she could tell me something useful, I would give her a rise in wages.—8 Feb

Charlotte sat at her dressing table for some time after she had returned to her room. Her maid had squealed with astonishment when she saw her mistress's hair, though she had not yet discerned whether or not she approved. It was amazing to Charlotte that something as simple as a change in hair could affect so much difference. However, the same could be said of Sir David. Had she not known it was him, very likely she would not have looked twice.

She shook her curls from side to side, relishing the freedom from the heavy weight she had carried for years. Would he notice the change?

"You must banish the silly, romantic girl inside, Charlotte," she told her reflection.

It was a difficult task when he had awakened the dormant passions inside her...and then spurned her when next he saw her. Yet there was something about his actions which belied his words and gave her a flicker of hope; made her wonder. He had made no promises—only warnings—so why did it hurt so much? Most would call it calf-love, her first infatuation. But no other man, with his mere presence, had caused her pulse to race or her insides to feel as though a swift was fluttering its wings inside her.

Standing, she walked to the balcony, looking up to the sliver of a moon, the peppering of stars twinkling across the sky and the clouds rushing by. They would forever have more meaning to her. She opened the door and a rush of cold air whipped her in the face. She welcomed the harsh reality. It was time to stop going through life in a haze of fantasies.

Inhaling deeply of the cold, salty sea air, she closed her eyes and leaned her forehead against the cold window, wishing for things that could never be. At least she had been kissed. That would have to carry her through the remainder of her days.

A derisive laugh escaped her when she thought of how she used to pray to the heavens for someone to love her, and to be kissed before she died. It was not enough, yet it had to be. David was right. There was no future in that quarter.

Change was definitely the order of the day. There was no chance of going back to the contentment she had felt before.

Another gust of frigid air reminded her that she was underdressed for moonlight reflections outside, and she was tightening her wrapper when she heard voices. She glanced at the clock; its hands ticking ever nearer three of the clock!

Was that Yardley, welcoming Sir David inside?

Charlotte gasped as an idea floated through her mind. Did she dare force her brother's hand? She was no schemer and could not coherently think through the repercussions of her actions, but she was well-read enough to consider this to be a golden opportunity.

Checking herself in the mirror with a slight pang of doubt, she took a deep breath, grabbed her candle and hurried downstairs to fetch a book to…aid her insomnia.

As she reached the bottom of the stairs, the door to the library opened and she could not stop her momentum before she crashed into a hard, male chest. Large, warm arms surrounded her and a hushing sound fell into her ears. One arm left her and she heard the door to the library latch. She looked up to find piercing grey eyes watching her like a hungry wolf.

"What are you doing here?" she asked quietly, while savouring the feel of his arms around her.

He shook his head. "I must go. We cannot be seen together," he said, as though trying to convince himself. Slowly he released her.

She wrinkled her forehead.

"The Duke is in there," he whispered, inclining his head toward the library.

She still did not quite understand what the fuss was about. Yardley was just her brother. Without a word, she took David's hand and led him to her small, private parlour at the back of the house.

"Lady Charlotte…" His voice was laced with warning. "I cannot be here."

She noticed him diverting his eyes. Suddenly she recalled her state of dishabille and blushed.

"You have cut your hair," he observed, reaching up to tenderly finger a curl.

She swallowed hard and watched his face as he realized what he had done. He pulled his hand back as though he had touched a hot iron.

"Y-yes. Why are you so concerned to be seen with me? If Yardley can be friendly with you, then why can I not?"

"How can you ask such a thing? He is my employer. We were just discussing estate concerns."

"At three of the clock in the morning?"

"He was at the funeral."

"And the business cannot wait until later?" she asked doubtfully.

"I noticed some smuggling on the beach on my way home from the inn and happened upon him at the stables."

She narrowed her gaze. So he spent his evenings in the village, at the public house. Why was she not surprised, yet still hurt? No doubt he favoured those tavern wenches who were no better than they ought to be.

"You need not dine there. You are welcome at our table, regardless of your employment; you are family to our guests."

"I could not, my lady."

"You could!" she insisted. "Are you in some kind of trouble that you must hide?"

"Nothing for you to concern yourself over."

She forced herself not to pout and crossed her arms over her chest, feeling self-conscious as he was obviously going to reject her again. Something was going on that he refused to tell her. "Would you rather tell me what this is about or should I ask my brother? Do I not have the right to know?"

"You do not understand what you are asking." He ran his fingers through his dark locks, leaving them adorably ruffled. "I must stay away from you. Good night, my lady." He bowed and began to leave the room.

"Wait!"

He hesitated at the door before turning to look back at her.

Suddenly she did not feel so brave, but she had to know. "If things were different…"

A look of tenderness softened his face for a moment as she held her breath for the answer. He shook his head. "But they are not." He closed the door behind him.

Frustration mounting, Charlotte picked up a cushion and threw it at the door behind him, trying not to sob. Instead, she marched out of the door back to the library with every intention of confronting Yardley, but the room was shrouded in darkness. He had already retired.

"Of course he is already upstairs," she muttered to herself. "He goes to his wife and I go to my books."

She held up her taper to light her way and went straight for her favourite novel, *Persuasion*. The bindings were well worn, as a proper book should be. If she were to write a book, she could think of no finer compliment. Perhaps that is what her purpose in life was—to tell stories. But where would she start? Keeping a journal was one thing, while weaving a novel was akin to an artist wielding a paintbrush.

Leaning her forehead against the bookshelf, she had to fight back despair. She knew she was fortunate...there were so many with so little and she had so much... Why could she not be satisfied? Even her favourite tale of romance could not erase the anguish in her heart.

A scratching sound from behind the wall caused her to jump and squeal.

"It is only a mouse," she told herself as she tried to still the frantic beat of her heart. "That is why you do not go through the house alone at night," she reminded herself as she hurried from the library and returned to her room. "And there are three lazy mousers who need to earn their keep," she pronounced to said beasts, who barely opened an eye to the intruder.

DAVID CHUCKLED when he heard the object hit the door behind him, so he stayed in the shadows and waited. He watched as Lady Charlotte marched to the library to do heaven knew what, and then continued to watch as she carried on a conversation with herself.

There was more to the lady than she revealed—he had to restrain himself from going in after her. She was temptation itself in her wrapper, which showed that she possessed a far more alluring figure than intimated by those awful dresses she wore.

For some reason, Lady Charlotte was determined to see him dead, for Yardley would have his neck and not be so jovial if he knew he was still talking with his sister—and pining for her—in the middle of the night. Reluctantly, he let himself out of the servants' door and walked back to his cottage to indulge in sweet dreams of Lady Charlotte. For dreams were all that could ever be between them. Hopefully, she would come to see it as well before she drove him completely mad.

Later the next day, David found the Duke in the paddock with Dido and Gulliver. His Grace had left a note for David to wait on him at his convenience.

"Good day, your Grace."

"Douglas." Yardley inclined his head from where he stood, against the fence, watching the mare and stallion prance around each other.

"She and Gulliver will have some fine offspring."

"I expect Dido to be in heat soon. She is still warning him off while at the same time showing him she is interested." Yardley glanced at David. "I spoke with Jeffries this morning. He knew more of the vicar. It seems Howard comes from minor gentry on his father's side, but his mother's family owns a munitions manufactory."

David considered the implications. "As a smuggler, my mind is turning with possibilities. Munitions are a thriving business, with the constant advances in design, not to mention the recent wars. However, the profits would be at least doubled if gained illegally."

"Money is the root of all evil," Yardley proffered.

"Or the lack thereof," David retorted. "But perhaps we have found the missing link? Our good vicar uses his occupation to avoid suspicion, and sends his family's goods out on the empty ships."

"Did you see crews sending cargo out?"

"I did not, but I was not looking for it, either. Exporting cargo is not the usual way, though it has been known to happen. Guns and ammunition are one thing England is superior at, though the thought of arming our enemies sickens me."

"Indeed. To my knowledge, our only major conflicts are in Africa, though it would not surprise me to find any of our adversaries keen to get their hands on more weapons," Yardley said.

"I did not find any stores of weapons or guns, though I had to choose only one spot to scout last night. Did your steward know of the tunnel to Langborn? I can trace it now. They will be moving the goods tonight or the next and I would like to see if there is anything else to learn on that front."

"Jeffries mentioned there used to be a tunnel which led to a hidden storeroom behind the library, which was sealed in my father's time. He also thought there was a storage vault under the conservatory, but he has not looked in there in two decades."

"Would you mind if I looked around later?"

"Not at all. There might even be some creatures hiding, for your pleasure," Yardley added with a sardonic grin.

"Speaking of which, I thought I heard some mice last night. I suppose that is my purview, though some good mouser cats would be my preference. I imagine what we are looking for either went out last night or goes on another shipment. I need to find out who the agent is, which means I need to insinuate myself into the gang quickly."

"The thought of you in church warms my insides," Yardley teased. "I cannot wait to hear Howard's sermon. 'Tis interesting the good vicar chose to keep his hand in the minor goods. Could it be a diversion?"

"Aye, that it could. They have quite an operation, with some walking as bold as brass up the high street to the inn, carrying gin. Tea and lace went through the tunnel to the church, and I suspect there is more elsewhere."

"If you need more help, you only have to ask," Yardley remarked with a sincere look. "I have sent word to my agent in London, to see if he can discover anything more about Howard."

"One thing that kept plaguing me about the smuggling run was the absence of Captain Dunn."

"What do you think is happening?"

"I am not certain, but perhaps they are loading from the water. Is there a dock nearby?"

"Brighton is the closest port for large ships. I keep a yacht there for the occasional trip to the Continent."

"That might prove to be quite useful if my suspicions are correct."

"I will have it made ready to be at your disposal."

"I do appreciate your assistance in this matter. I am quite anxious to settle it."

"I have a stake in this as well."

"Still...it would be much more difficult without your assistance and resources."

The Duke nodded and looked back at the horses, clearly uncomfortable with this gratitude.

"I suppose I will have to make my way towards Brighton and look over the docks."

"The ladies are going to Brighton to look for fabrics. Her Grace has decided to make my sister and your niece her projects for this Season," Yardley remarked.

David knew they had convinced his sister to go out, and that was no small feat since her injury. "Her Grace must be a force of nature if she talked my sister and niece into any sort of outing. My sister sent me a note, asking me to help her this morning."

"Jolie has that effect on people." The Duke smiled fondly. David's initial impression of Yardley had been that of a pompous donkey's hind end, but more and more he was liking the fellow. Cavenray had also surprised him. David knew, if he managed his way out of this conundrum, it would be because of their help. It was a humbling thought.

"Then I should also mention she ordered me to attend dinner at the house, two evenings from now."

Yardley's head snapped back at him. "I beg your pardon? What is she up to now?"

"I am not the one to question, sir, but I do not think it would be wise."

"Indeed not."

CHAPTER 9

There is nothing more humiliating to a plump girl than the modiste. So what is it called when she must go with the century's greatest beauty? Insufferable. Every time, the seamstress points out my flaws as if I could not see them for myself. At least none have told me I am better suited to the stage...to my face.
—9 Feb

"I must insist that you come!" Jolie was speaking to Lady Brennan as Charlotte entered the breakfast parlour the next morning.

"I do not go out in public any more. Besides, it is such an effort to transport this contraption that it is not to be thought of." Lady Brennan indicated her wheeled chair with a wave of her hand.

"It is no trouble at all. Getting out of the house will be good for all of us. I cannot abide being closeted indoors for more than a day or two."

"Then the three of you should go for a ride. It is of no matter to me to stay here and do my exercises and read a book. The library here is full of novels I have yet to read."

Charlotte could feel herself blushing, but Lady Brennan did not seem to think the abundance of novels there was scandalous, as many of her station would.

"We must go to Brighton for fabrics. Letty and Charlotte both need some new gowns."

"I do not need new gowns, your Grace," Letty objected.

"Yes, you do, my dear. I insist you have a wardrobe fit for any occasion, as does your brother," Lady Brennan said gently.

Letty visibly struggled to control her features and Charlotte could see that they had argued much over this topic. "Very well, Mama, but only if you come with us."

"You know why I cannot."

"And you know why I choose not to, but I think it is time we faced the *ton*. I cannot believe Society's treatment of us could be worse than our fear of it."

"Hear, hear." Jolie applauded. "I have weathered a scandal myself, and I agree with Letty, it is best to get on with it. It will blow over quickly with all of the support you will have. Cavenray recognizes her, and you wish for her to make a good match, no?"

"Of course I do. But I would wish for her to choose as her heart desires, so she is not tempted to make the poor choices I did."

"Oh, Mama. Is that what you wish for me?"

Lady Brennan had averted her face, trying to control her emotions, but she nodded.

"Very well. I will go."

"Excellent!" Jolie clapped her hands with excitement.

None of the Ashbury ladies were to be denied when they set their mind to something, Charlotte mused, watching the play unfold before her.

"I do think we should hold a small entertainment here to give Letty a chance to have a taste of Society. Nothing outrageous, of course. Lord and Lady Wyndham are still in mourning."

"I suppose a small affair would be acceptable," Lady Brennan conceded, "but I do not ever plan to go into London Society again."

Jolie smiled and said nothing more. Charlotte knew that smile, however, and she also knew Jolie to be an excellent strategist. She had won this battle and she would be patient to win the war. For some reason, Jolie wanted Letty to succeed, and who would not once they had met her? But Charlotte suspected Jolie intended them to do the social whirl together and Charlotte could sacrifice herself for her friend one more time. She had done it many Seasons before, after all.

"I will have the carriages sent for so we may be to Brighton early. They are expecting us," Jolie said with a mischievous wink as she strolled through the door.

Soon, two carriages were brought round, one for the ladies and one carrying Lady Brennan's chair and her nurse. What surprised Charlotte most of all was that Sir David was there, carrying Lady Brennan to the carriage.

Strangely, no one acted as though they knew him. While they stood waiting, he placed her gently inside the carriage and Lady Brennan kissed her brother on the cheek when she likely thought no one could see. He gave his sister's hand a quick squeeze in return. Charlotte's heart nearly melted inside her chest.

Was everyone in on this scheme but her? She was about to ask out of frustration, but something about Letty's expression gave her pause. Perhaps Lady Brennan did not know about her brother not being pardoned. How could she not know of his reduced circumstances dressed as he was? And did they all think to hide it from her? Had Lady Brennan not been present, Charlotte would have confronted Jolie and Letty. Yardley never kept anything from his wife, and Charlotte was quite certain Jolie was scheming about something...and why was she so suspicious of everyone now? It was unsettling.

Sir David handed them, one by one, into the carriage, acting the gentleman—or footman—for each of them. He kept his eyes averted as he handed her in, while she barely kept her hand from trembling at his touch. Jolie stepped back and spoke with him a moment before she joined them. Charlotte was burning with curiosity to know what she had said to him. One thing was certain: Jolie knew the supposed servant was Sir David.

The more secretive everyone was, the more Charlotte's interest burned. It was enough to make her contemplate doing outrageous, unladylike things. She desperately wished she and Jolie were alone, so she could pry information from the Duchess, but it would be hours before she had the opportunity. Instead, she was doing her least favourite activity in the world: going to the modiste.

A GROOM HAD Gulliver saddled and waiting for David after he saw the ladies off to Brighton. How he longed to tell Lady Charlotte the whole! The look in her eyes was going to be the death of him. If only he could make matters progress more quickly, he could remove himself from this millstone which was causing him to sink in more ways than one.

It was a surprisingly mild day for February as he first made his way into the village of Rottingdean. When Cook happened to hear of his destination, she asked him to order some extra meat from the butcher for the gathering the Duchess was planning. It was a chance to see more of the village during the day and to determine other good hiding spots. To a smuggler, everywhere had potential. Turning down the High Street, people watched him with curiosity and he tipped his hat in an effort to be friendly. He had no doubt, as he tethered Gulliver to a post in front of the shop, that most of them were involved in the free trade in one way or another.

As he was about to enter the butcher's shop, he heard voices across the street and recognized one of them as the Revenue Officer. Another man looked like a naval officer, though older, and a third was a middle-aged army colonel. They entered the inn across the street, he noted, and decided he would make his way there next for a bite to eat.

When he entered the shop, he was surprised to find himself faced with Captain Dunn, behind the counter slicing a side of beef with a large knife.

"What can I do for you...sir?" Dunn asked suspiciously.

"Name's Douglas. I am new at Langborn. Mrs. Headly asked if you could send a large ham over for a gathering on Friday night."

"Aye, I can do that." He wiped his bloody knife on his apron. "What are you doing at Langborn? You smell like a gent."

David feigned indifference. He knew this was his moment. "I was brought up a gentleman, but it did not work out. I have spent the last decade in the Indies, forgetting my roots."

Dunn eyed him thoughtfully while gnawing a piece of straw. "Mayhap you can be useful here sometimes."

"I have some experience of being useful. Happens to be why I like to lie low."

Dunn smiled deviously, his crooked, yellow teeth showing. "'Twas you who let out the warning the other night, eh?"

David shrugged. "Never could stomach a man being hanged for feeding his family."

The butcher grunted approval. "I ain't worried much about Officer Nibley. You any good at climbing or sailing?"

"Both," he answered confidently, understanding the operation better and better by the moment. "It seems my employer would not mind my being useful either. He mentioned some tunnels and hinted at their sitting empty."

"This Duke likes his brandy, eh?"

"I am certain there is an amicable arrangement to be made."

"I'll talk it over with my associates. Meet me at the Black Horse tomorrow night and I'll tell you what they say."

"I will be there." David looked out of the window and saw the two officers standing near Gulliver. "Are there many of their sort 'round here?"

Dunn looked up and narrowed his gaze at the Excise men. "Enough to be a bloody nuisance. They been joining up with the navy, since they got nothing better to do these days."

"Mm." David muttered his agreement then took his leave, making his way slowly to his horse, hoping to hear something useful. He was not ready to approach the Revenue men, even with the King's authority, for fear it would compromise his position. He kept his hat down low and fiddled with his saddlebags, trying to listen.

"Are you certain it is not a dummy run? The last three times there have been nothing but fishermen," the navy man said quietly yet with obvious frustration.

"Of course I cannot be certain! I do not have reliable sources nor enough men to keep a look-out, but I swear they are loading in the water, and I cannot be here and there!"

"Very well, I will send out a patrol on Sunday night. Pray you will be right this time."

"I am afraid I cannot justify extra men on the ground until there is more concrete evidence," the army man added.

David unhooked Gulliver's reins from the post and led him away before the men turned around. He walked two streets away before mounting and heading west. If they were planning a big run for Sunday night, they had to have the goods stored nearby. He only had three days to find them.

There was little but farmland during the few miles to Brighton. The King's Pavilion, with its odd architecture, stood out amongst the growing seaside resort. It was a shame, from the looks of the King recently. It did not appear he would be enjoying this extravagance much longer.

He left Gulliver at a posting house, and proceeded on foot the rest of the way. The town was flourishing, with new construction of terrace houses, and the streets were teeming with people shopping, merchants and vendors. Ladies and gentlemen were strolling along the promenade and pier—a smaller version of London, it seemed. He could only imagine how crowded it would be in the summertime.

The English Channel was full of ships, both merchant and naval, and it was difficult to clearly determine the intended purpose of each. He descended the steps from the pier, walking along the pebbled beach as though out for a stroll. Fishermen were hauling in their catches and cleaning their nets; gulls squealed and squawked as they soared through the air.

He stood with his hand shielding his eyes as he surveyed the various boats and ships, trying not to cover his nose while he acclimated to the stench from the dead fish. At last, he spotted Yardley's schooner—unsurprisingly named *The Jolie*—which bobbed in the water, anchored with furled masts, indicating it was abandoned for the winter or whims of its master. Most of the others were in obvious use, as he suspected his quarry would be. He thrust his hands in his pockets. What would he do if it were his operation?

"'Oo ye lookin' fer?"

David looked down to see a weathered old man whom he had overlooked, sitting amongst some rocks.

"Just checking on my master's ship while I was passing through town."

"The Dook's?"

"Aye. He had word that it was being used without his knowledge." David risked being unmasked to make up a plausible excuse.

"Tha's right. I seen it makin' runs to Shoreham an' back. Even east 'o here a time er two."

"How often have you noticed it?" David tried not to appear too anxious for information.

The man scrunched up his face to think, revealing a mouth devoid of his front teeth. "Mebbe once er twice a month 'te past several."

David considered this man very likely saw a good deal and was overlooked as being unworthy of notice. He handed the man a gold sovereign. "There is more where that came from if you happen to see who is using his Grace's ship."

He was not surprised when the old man bit down on the coin in appreciation.

"'An 'ow am I s'posed 'te tell ye 'iffin I see sumptin?"

David handed him another coin. "Leave a message with Mr. Attree, the solicitor on Ship Street."

"Aye aye, sir."

David inclined his head and made his way back to Gulliver, pondering just who he might be dealing with; who would be bold enough to appropriate his Grace's private yacht for nefarious purposes. It had to be either someone very sly or very stupid.

CHAPTER 10

Whoever would think knowing horses would be of benefit in torturing unwanted suitors? I wonder how much more fun I could have had this past decade if I had been so carefree?—10 Feb

$\mathcal{A}$ few days later, while dressing for the dinner party, Charlotte donned one of her new gowns and had to admit she did look as though she had an hourglass shape. The new style favoured the natural waist and she no longer resembled a large potato from the neck down. Though daily rides were making her stronger, she could not quite mask the abundance of bosom with which she had been blessed, nor the bottom to balance it out—regardless of whichever body-contorting corset the modiste recommended. She was now old enough to wear bolder colours, and Jolie had wasted no time in helping her choose darker hues. Tonight, she picked the cerulean blue, which made her eyes a vibrant blue-green rather than their usual resemblance to dirty Channel water. The décolleté left much to be desired, in her humble opinion, and also left little to the imagination. It was only family and friends there tonight, regretfully.

"There you are!" Jolie exclaimed as she waltzed through the door, dashing all of Charlotte's thoughts of her own pleasing appearance in comparison. Jolie wore a violet gown that made her exotic eyes of the same colour more striking. She was eyeing Charlotte with approval and that was enough to satisfy her. "Are you pleased?"

"I think it is an improvement, and that is agreeable," Charlotte murmured with feigned indifference.

"I invited Sir David," Jolie said in an off-hand manner.

"I beg your pardon?" Charlotte whirled around to face her. "You mean the new gamekeeper who everyone pretends they do not know?"

"*Oui.* I told Benedict you would recognize him, but he insists we cannot call him by his name." Jolie was half-French and it exhibited itself in her mannerisms and speech from time to time.

"Did he accept the dinner invitation?" Charlotte asked, twirling a lock of hair, hoping her anxiety did not show.

"No, and Benedict scolded me for asking him."

"Oh. Benedict could do with some scolding himself." Charlotte could not mask her disappointment. "Do you know why Sir David is working here? Have his circumstances changed so drastically that he is reduced to seeking employment?"

"Benedict spouted some rubbish about his needing a place until his pardon. I still do not see why we must call him Douglas and act as though he is a servant, especially when Letty and Lady Brennan are here."

"Did you see how they ignored him earlier? I do not understand! He also told me I must not acknowledge him!"

"You spoke with him?" Jolie's curiosity was written on her face.

Charlotte knew she was flushing. "He happened upon me when Minerva went lame."

"And?" Her eyes widened with interest.

"And nothing. He examined the horse's injury and then led her back to the stables."

"How disappointing."

"Indeed," she agreed. "When I confronted him, he told me to forget him. Yet I would swear he did not truly mean it. Not that I am an expert in such matters."

"Well, I think him quite suitable. We will just have to convince Benedict."

"What do you mean?"

"Oh, your stubborn sibling forbade Sir David to see you."

"He did what?" Charlotte felt a flash of temper. How dare he interfere? But of course he would—it was his birthright! Charlotte would need no rouge for her cheeks tonight!

Jolie, seemingly not sensing the fire coursing through Charlotte's veins, made her way to the door. "Oh, I almost forgot. Benedict invited a few of his acquaintances to dinner. He mentioned you might be interested. Something about an agreement?" She tilted her head curiously, then smiled before floating away with the ethereal grace the ladies in her family were born with.

Charlotte stopped at Letty's room to see if she was ready to go to the drawing room, but her chamber was empty. Continuing on down the stairs, Charlotte clamped her jaw as she pondered who her brother would choose for her, and resolved to be polite. Who would he think suitable? A forty-year-old widower with six young children? Or a jolly, balding, slightly pudgy man with ruddy cheeks? No, even Yardley would not think her that motherly. A scholarly type who collected artefacts from ancient Egypt? A tall, thin gentleman, perhaps, with spectacles and dishevelled hair when he was concentrating. Charlotte did not approve of concentrating too hard or taking anything too seriously, for that matter. He might be a possibility if he was independently wealthy, nevertheless. Benedict would not welcome a parasite only wishing funds for his projects.

She stopped. Who would *she* think suitable? A tall, swarthy man who looked like a pirate and gave swash-buckling kisses, of course. She laughed out loud and almost skipped down the stairs.

A large smile still lightened her face as she entered the drawing room, to stop short when she met with three strange gentlemen. Three strange, handsome-enough gentlemen stood regarding her. They were all younger than forty, she suspected, but did they have all of their teeth? Her gaze searched the room for her brother, who was watching her with an unnatural gleam of amusement in his eye. Well, maybe it was natural for a brother who took pleasure in torturing a little sister. She gave him a slight narrowing of her eyes, a code between siblings meaning *you will pay for this later*. His response? A wink! He was fortunate there were strangers here or she would unleash her fury in unladylike terms!

He took a smooth sip from his glass and made his way towards her. When confronted with young, handsome strangers, the old Charlotte's palms grew sweaty and her tongue turned to jam. The new Charlotte would not allow it. She would pretend they were her nieces and nephews and be jolly. Heaven only knew, the shy, quiet lady had not worked well in Society.

"Charlotte, you remember Captain Harris, of course."

Lady Olivia's husband. No, she had not recognized the younger Captain Harris out of uniform, but his dark good looks were familiar. She held out her hand to him. "A pleasure to see you again, sir."

"Likewise, Lady Charlotte."

One down, two to go. She turned to the next gentleman. He was average in appearance—much like any other English aristocrat, with his thinning blond hair and pale blue eyes—but he had a very kind smile and his demeanour instantly put Charlotte at ease. He was introduced as Mr. Davenport, the shipping magnate, and an old school friend. Even she had heard of Davenport Shipping.

"Mr. Davenport." She inclined her head. He bowed in acknowledgement.

The third gentleman was as tall as the Duke but more intimidating. That was because she did not know him, but his height was equal to her brother's and his dark eyes and dark hair made her think of the devil.

"And this, sister dear, is the renowned Colonel Prescott."

Well, she had never heard of him, but that did not mean much.

"Delighted, Colonel."

"Charmed, Lady Charlotte," he said with a scowl that appeared to be a permanent feature from the deep lines etched on his face. Perhaps it was his normal look, but she pitied his soldiers. She stood to the side, allowing the men to continue their conversation.

No, she still did not feel instantly at ease as she had with Sir David. She smiled and tried to be amiable to the new gentlemen, but the whole time her mind was swirling with possibilities of how to make Sir David eligible. If her brother was the main obstacle, then he would have to be overcome.

What was Sir David doing instead of having dinner with them? She envisioned him down at the Black Horse, slicing into a slab of mutton and being fawned over by a serving girl. Feeling her face assume a frown, she forced her features back to neutral.

There had to be more to the story than she was being told, she decided, as she twirled one of her new short curls. It was becoming a habit, she noticed, dropping her hand away again. It simply did not make sense for Sir David to approach Yardley for help when he had his own powerful relatives to assist him, or would he feel too much shame? Charlotte would have to find out the answers. It seemed she must take her future in her own hands or her brother might put it in the hands of someone like Prescott.

Lord and Lady Wyndham were announced, followed shortly by the newly wedded Duke and Duchess of Cavenray. Langborn had not held this many visitors in decades.

"Maili!" Charlotte welcomed her friend.

"We came to visit after our wedding trip, and arrived at Wyndham to visit Lady Brenham only to hear the sad news," the Duchess replied, kissing her cheek.

"Yes, indeed. Now I wish to know every last detail," Charlotte said, linking arms with Maili and keeping her engrossed until the butler announced dinner was served.

Dinner was not overly tedious, despite Charlotte being seated between the two new gentlemen. She almost felt sorry for them, but Benedict had probably bribed them with mating a horse or lured them with her obscene dowry, which he kept increasing. Letty was seated next to Davenport and her brother, Cavenray, so at least she was spared flirting for part of the time. Thankfully, the food was superb, she reflected as she sipped on white soup. She first turned to the partner on her right, Colonel Prescott.

89

"What brings you to Langborn, sir?" Charlotte barely managed to keep a straight face as she pondered dinner topics. If she was going to be uncomfortable, then so were her perspective suitors. She was loath to make small talk with him, though she was tempted to try to wipe his perpetual scowl from his face.

He cast an uncomfortable glance toward Yardley, then met her gaze. "Your brother invited me for a visit, of course. A tedious business; nothing to interest you, I am sure."

"Have you come to look over the stock? Does it meet with your approval?" She would not be deterred so easily.

He raised his eyebrows in shock. What had she said?

"It is much too soon to comment. Choosing...stock is very personal."

Did he mean horses or mates? Amused, Charlotte persisted. "Oh, the *stock* here is quite above average, sir."

"So your brother has intimated," he replied pompously, taking a sip of wine.

"Fine teeth," She smiled. "Deep girth." She demonstrated with her hands. "Fine legs with sufficient bone for the purpose..." She thought he would have a spasm as his face turned a deep shade of red.

"Impeccable lineage, of course."

She inclined her head. "And the price is...right."

"And disposition?" he asked. Was he catching on?

"Oh, nothing placid, to be sure," she said with a saucy grin. "And the ride, you will have to judge for yourself."

She turned to her other side before he had time to react, trying not to burst out laughing.

Mr. Davenport and Letty appeared to be getting on well, Charlotte noticed with relief as she waited for him to turn to her. If rumours were true, he had no need of her dowry and Letty was sister to a duke as well, if connections were his aim. Charlotte had no interest in connections or either of these gentleman for matches.

Neither of them made her feel the way Sir David did.

Selecting a fillet of fowl *a la bechamelle,* she was still feeling a bit devilish from her conversation with Prescott as she turned to Davenport.

"How are you enjoying Sussex thus far, sir? Are you also here to peruse the breeding stock?" She could not help but grin mischievously.

Davenport caught on quickly. "Ah, I could not help but overhear some of your conversation with Prescott," he leaned in and murmured in a low voice. "I fear the poor man boasts no humour."

"He had no warning, I am afraid. It was badly done of me," she said, unrepentant. "I really ought not take out frustrations with my brother's marital schemes for me on the unsuspecting."

"You would be quite unappreciated with him." Davenport agreed, his eyes twinkling.

"Pray, tell me what my brother lured you here with," she asked, hoping her fellow conspirator would indulge her curiosity.

"Only excellent company, I assure you." His lips twitched.

Charlotte sent him a glance of exasperated amusement. "Should you ever desire a future in politics, sir, I happen to know a well-connected duke."

Davenport laughed. "I will keep that in mind, my lady."

"Do return your efforts to Miss Dickerson. She is well worth your trouble." Charlotte turned her attention to the trifle being placed before her, wishing she could have such easy conversation with men she had true interest in.

Once the covers were removed and they left the gentleman to their port, Charlotte decided it was time to get some answers.

But how? Everyone was determined to be so secretive! Was she a child to be sheltered from the truth? If it was so horrid she would rather hear it now than after her heart was irreparably damaged.

THE NIGHT WAS clear and cold, and the moon was waxing, but bright enough to scare away any smuggler who feared the Revenue. With little shelter and a backdrop of white chalk, this was not an ideal place for the free trade, with officers on your heels, yet David knew something large was happening here. He had just left the Black Horse, where he had been welcomed warily and instructed on the next run of gin and tea. Not that he expected to be told all their dark secrets at the beginning; he must earn their trust. He was growing impatient, however, to have this ruse over and be freed.

There had been talk about diversions for the Revenue Officers, which was the usual game played. David only listened with half an ear to that part. Dummy ships were sent out, lots of false information was spread, and often bribes were paid. It sounded harmless enough that they were planning to move the trail markers the new officer had placed about to guide his way. There were several good laughs and toasts drunk to foolish Excisemen. Hopefully, the officer was clever enough not to place his markers right along the cliff's edge. David waited for any hints of other places they might be storing munitions, but he heard nothing he did not already know. Disappointed, he finished his ale and left.

He and Gulliver walked slowly back from the village. He was not looking forward to returning to his cold, lonely cottage. There were still lights on at the main house, and he reckoned the dinner must still be going on. Would he rather be there, wining and dining with the nobility, than doing this? A difficult question, as he preferred neither. He did not belong in either place now. He did wish to be with Lady Charlotte, however, which was why this adventure needed to move faster. He was unable to bear the pleading look in her eyes much longer.

He laughed out loud. If she felt half the attraction he did, it was dangerous to be in the same Shire! He should leave for Barbados as soon as this was finished. He must see this through for his own self-worth, but he could not see a good end to it, or at least not one that would allow him to be the husband Lady Charlotte deserved.

Husband? What madness was this? That particular word, in relation to himself, had never crossed his thoughts—and it should not now! They had hardly had a chance to know one another, but they had an unimaginable connection.

He dismounted from Gulliver and walked him into the stables. Dido nickered to Gulliver as he led him past the stalls. David could sympathize with the mare. He wanted to be with his mate as well.

After removing the saddle and harness and rubbing the stallion down, although he began walking down the path to his cottage, his feet took him towards the gardens. What did he intend to do? Look in the windows like a thief or Peeping Tom, coveting something he could not have? His mind kept telling him he was searching for the old tunnels, but his heart hoped for a glimpse of Lady Charlotte. Why was he making such a fool of himself over this woman? He had given up hope long ago of a traditional relationship bound by holy matrimony. Nothing about him was traditional, since he had chosen this selfish path as a youth.

All he could hope to do at this point was clear his name. He wandered around the gardens, looking for any sign of hiding places. He was fairly good at seeing what others would overlook. There was a long conservatory at the back of the house; beyond it lay a formal garden, followed by another series of succession houses. It was an unusual arrangement, but perhaps one of the ladies was a gardening enthusiast. Pebbled paths were lined with yews, elders and hawthorns. He wished he had looked by day. He walked around the perimeter of the further buildings and found what looked to be an entrance at the side of the ice house wall. It no doubt led nowhere other than to the ice, but he decided he might as well look while he was here. He took the lantern hanging on the nail by the door and lit the flint before descending.

As David suspected, there was a door at the bottom of the well which had been dug out for ice. It did not appear to have been opened in decades, however, by the look of the layers of dirt and rust. He set the lantern down at his feet and began to prise at the door latch, but it would not budge. Taking his blade from his boot, he scraped and chipped at the decay surrounding the lock. With some skill and diligence, he was able to force it open. It was not enough, and he had to chip away the elements jamming the door before he had success.

Clearly, this was not the route of entry if there was any storage taking place here at Langborn.

After much effort, the door finally gave way with a loud creaking sound. He stepped inside and heard the door slam in place behind him with a bang that echoed through the tunnel. The flame flickered from the gust and he whirled around and cursed himself. He should have paid more attention. Down on the floor was a rock, which should have been used to hold the door open. He prayed there would be a way out at the other end, or he would not be found before it was too late.

Not willing to concede defeat or panic yet, he began to walk gingerly through the tunnel, dodging cobwebs and who knew what else on the wet, slippery floor. The familiar scents of must and mould intermixed with the sounds of dripping water and scampering rodents. After about twenty yards, he found the tunnel split in two directions. He chose the path to the left, suspecting it would lead to the conservatory. He was met with another door, which showed the same signs of disuse as the other. Turning back, he followed the second path another fifty yards. This door, while old, had been used recently. His pulse sped up with anticipation as it used to when he was young—the thrill of being chased, doing something secretive, making large profits—he was still not wholly immune to an adventure, though now he would choose a different way to fulfil the urge.

He held up the lantern and looked around, investigating for other signs of use. Someone was very, very careful, and had swept behind themselves. He found a track that had been missed, leaving half a footprint and a partial wheel print.

The lock on this door appeared to be new, and was unable to be picked without damaging it. He did not wish to alert the gang that he was searching for them. He turned and made his way back the way he had come, looking for the turn to the beach. He was surprised there was yet another fork in the path and he was certain he could not have stumbled all the way to the Saltdean Gap yet. Had another tunnel been forged or was this underground system much more intricate than they had known? It was all quite disorientating!

The tunnel made a sharp turn to the left and David had a difficult time keeping his sense of direction in the dark. He had not paced out his steps, as he normally did, to keep his bearings. Growing worried over what he might encounter, he hid his light underneath his cloak when he sensed he approached the entrance to the beach. Creeping slowly, he stopped to allow his eyes to adjust—but what he saw astonished him.

There was a small ravine which emptied out to the Channel. Two small skiffs bobbed in the water, almost hidden. It was a smuggler's dream. Was there any possible way Yardley was not complicit in this operation? He had to know of this ravine. He ran his hand through his hair with frustration. How could he free himself without causing problems for Yardley or Lady Charlotte?

He climbed back up the edge of the cliff, and was grateful for his years of climbing experience, for it was a steep and slippery climb. Breathing heavily by the time he reached the top, he debated going inside and confronting Yardley, but knowing he had a house full of guests gave him pause.

He stopped at the conservatory and leaned against the ornate iron framework. He could hear the sound of music, reminding him of the abyss which separated himself from Lady Charlotte. He could picture her laughing and dancing, with gentleman hanging on her every witty word. Then he saw her standing there, looking angelic with the glow of candlelight behind her golden hair. She stood not five feet from him, her fingers playing with the petals of an orchid through the streams of moisture running down the glass. It was an image worthy of being set to canvas, were he talented enough to capture the moment.

Watching her was wrong, but he could not look away. Like a moth drawn to a flame, it was a force he could not resist. An army officer entered the conservatory, apparently looking for her, and David's stomach curdled. Instead of staying to watch someone else court her, he decided to go in and wait to speak with Yardley.

CHAPTER 11

I am certain every lady feels oppressed by overbearing brothers. Add the monstrosity of a duke into the equation and it is untenable. Heaven forbid I make a mistake or have an original thought! Life was much, much simpler, when I was alone.—14 Feb

"I need to speak with you."

Yardley gave Charlotte his haughty, elder brother look. "Now? I have the men assembled in the study to discuss some important business. Can this not wait?"

"Surely they can drink brandy for five minutes?"

"Very well." He followed her into the library and closed the door behind him.

"I would like you to explain why you did not tell me Sir David was here."

"I did not see the point. He needs must lower himself to the station of a servant." He leaned against the edge of a desk and crossed his longs legs in front of him.

"His sister and niece are guests in our home."

"Everyone has a black sheep in their family. Would you like to explain why you are so concerned about Mr. Douglas?" Mockery edged his tone.

She looked away to hide her flush. "I have a suspicion you are hiding something from me."

"And I feel the same. You have cut your hair, you have changed your dress... are you, perchance, interested in Mr. Douglas? Is there something you are not telling me?"

"What if there is?" she asked, spreading her hands wide.

"He is not for you, Lottie."

"Who are you to decide my happiness?" she cried in outrage. Swinging away, she paced the dark blue and gold carpet.

"A doting older brother who knows much more of the world than you. And, in this case, much more of his story."

"Then please enlighten me." She sent him a dark glance.

"Why can you not be interested in a suitable gentleman? Davenport or Prescott, for instance?"

"Davenport only had eyes for Letty and Prescott is harder than cast-iron. Besides, can you imagine me following the drum?"

"The only drum you would have to follow is that of London Society. He sits at a desk at the Home Office."

"Do you mean to tell me you invited them here just to parade them as eligibles in front of me?" She placed her hands on her hips with exasperation.

"Actually, I called them here to aid me with a smuggling problem. Introducing them to you was an afterthought."

"Of course it was. What smuggling problem? They have never caused trouble before."

"I am not quite certain. It has come to the King's notice, however, and he wants it to cease immediately."

"How odd. So you have assembled this group of gentlemen, who are best suited to the task, with the expressed purpose of stopping the smugglers?"

He inclined his head. "Indeed."

"But what of the villagers? They need the supplemental income."

"I am afraid we will have to find another way. That is for another day. The gang is still operating and I have men awaiting my presence in the study."

He walked to her and placed his hands on her shoulders. Looking down into her eyes, he added in a brotherly tone, "Forget Douglas, Charlotte. He is dangerous. You must trust me to know what is best for you."

"It would be easier if you did not keep the details from me, your Grace."

"Your Grace?" His eyebrows elevated in offence.

"You are acting like a duke, not a brother," she explained with petulance, narrowing her eyes at him.

He smiled and kissed her on the forehead before leaving.

She barely managed to keep her face impassive until the door clicked behind him. She was a grown woman, not a child! How dare he treat her as though she could not handle the truth?

"And all in the name of brotherly love? Ha!" she declared, a laboured sigh escaping her.

Needing to release some frustration, she searched the library for something to pound, throw or break. There were no pillows to hand, and she groaned with irritation. "Why must I act like a lady? Does he not realize the more he tells me no, the more it makes me want it?"

She had to settle for pounding on the wall, and there was very little wall to be had in a room with floor to ceiling bookcases. There was a small amount of wood frame between each of the rows and rows of shelves. Pounding until her hand hurt, she then leaned against the fireplace, feeling foolish. Accidentally hitting her head on the metal sconce, she spun around to glare at the offending object. Then, catching her foot on the grate in the process, she overbalanced and grabbed hold of the sconce to steady herself. It snapped at the hinge and the wall began to move. Charlotte clung onto the mantel for dear life as the fireplace began to revolve and she found herself in a cold, dark room.

Shaking with fright, she whispered, "Where am I?" In alarm, she pushed hard against the fireplace, but nothing moved. There had to be a way back into the library! Thankful she was wearing gloves, she searched the wall in the darkness for a lever or other device, to no avail. Did the mechanism work only with the sconce?

With difficulty, she fought the instinct to panic as nothing she tried succeeded in opening the door. Shivering with a combination of the low temperature and morbid dread, she wrapped her arms around herself as tight as she could for warmth, and closed her eyes. She could not see and she was deathly afraid of spiders and anything else which crept or crawled. An unwanted memory played through her mind, of sitting in the library the other night and hearing a scratching sound. That meant there were mice or rats in here, as well as spiders.

How long would it be until someone found her? Would every one assume she had gone to bed?

"This cannot be happening. This cannot be happening. This cannot be happening. No, Chapman will be waiting for you. She knows you cannot remove this ridiculous new gown. But that could still be hours! If Benedict was to meet with the gentlemen, it might well be an age before the guests seek their chambers for the night," she muttered aloud.

The longer she stood there, the more afraid she became. Her mind began to fill with horrors from the various Gothic novels she had read. Ghosts, goblins, dragons and insane relatives locked away in dungeons were so much more amusing on the page. Every creak, whistle and scratch made her jump. Somewhere in the distance there was a constant drip, drip, drip. The unremitting rhythm of it made her want to scream. A chilly draught of air stroked her ankles, and then she noticed a door rattling far off in the blackness ahead. Where could the door be? And where did it lead? She tried to think where a tunnel could go to from here, but found it hard to conjecture in the smothering dark. She had always believed the old tunnels had been sealed during her father's time.

If only she had a light! "This is no less than I deserve for allowing myself to vent frustrations," she chastised, but it was too late for remorse.

Too afraid to step away from the revolving door lest she become lost or run into some terrible figment of her imaginings, she stayed where she was, huddled near the cold marble of the fireplace.

All she could do was hope someone would come searching for her in the library. If she had been able to hear the mice—she shuddered—then surely someone must hear her screams for help. In the meantime, she told herself fiercely, taking hold of the poker that was thankfully still in its place beside the grate, she would be brave. Still, she was not above praying she would not have to defend herself from rats.

~

"GENTLEMEN, I apologize for keeping you waiting. My sister had something important to discuss. I assume you have made yourselves acquainted with David Douglas?" Yardley inclined his head toward David. Wyndham, Prescott, Davenport and Cavenray all indicated their assent. David had been waiting when the rest of them had entered the study. All the gentlemen were seated in leather armchairs set in a half-circle around a large oak desk. Yardley took his seat behind it.

"He is here in the guise of my gamekeeper, the plan being to become a part of and then bring down the Rottingdean smuggling gang, at the request of our Sovereign. Douglas, would you mind apprising these gentlemen of what you have discovered so far?"

David explained his investigations to this point, including Captain Dunn and Reverend Howard's involvement, and that he suspected they were answering to someone else.

"Reverend Howard has family ties to a munitions manufactory, but I have seen no sign of stores of guns or ammunition. I have managed to insinuate myself into the gang, but have not been privy to anything other than the usual runs of lace and gin. I did overhear from the Revenue Officer that they suspect a large run to be taking place on Sunday night. That gives us two more days to discover any hiding places," David explained.

"I have asked each of you here," put in Yardley, "not at his request, but because I feel it behoves all of us to resolve this quickly. Colonel Prescott, do you have any information from the Home Office?"

"I was surprised by the secrecy surrounding this, especially given His Majesty has made such a request of Mr. Douglas. However, I did finally discover that it has to do with arms being sent out to our enemies illegally. Apparently, a bill is to be proposed, allowing arms to be sold to whomever has the wherewithal, regardless of their allegiance to Britain."

"To arm the very men who would kill us? Who would propose such a thing?" Wyndham asked, his voice rising in outrage.

"That is the answer I was unable to ascertain," Prescott answered.

"I did send word to have Howard investigated, but they only confirmed the connection. There is no proof they are distributing arms illegally. I have sent some men to keep an eye out nevertheless."

"Captain Harris, were you able to discover anything from the navy?" David asked.

"Patrols have been increased along the Channel, but it is difficult to be everywhere at once. It is impossible to check every boat coming in when you are an island nation. I did speak with Captain Garrick, and he also spoke of a suspected run they think to be bigger than usual, happening on Sunday night."

"My company was approached a few months ago, in connection with delivering arms to Asia. We turned down the business, not feeling comfortable with the destination of those armaments. There was something underhanded about the whole business," Davenport informed the gathering.

"Do you recall who approached you?"

"No, but I will question my secretary tomorrow."

"We must use our collective knowledge to discover where the contraband is being stored. There has to be somewhere nearby. They could not load a ship quickly if everything was not on hand," Lord Wyndham pointed out.

"I agree—having had first-hand knowledge of how smuggling works. They want that part of the operation done as quickly as possible."

"Captain Garrick did mention they have been sailing in circles following dummy runs. This gang is savvy," Harris observed.

"I believe they have been using Yardley's yacht to move the goods. This afternoon I discovered an old fisherman who had seen *The Jolie* being moved from Shoreham on more than one occasion."

Yardley cursed.

"I also explored the tunnels under your property, which you thought were sealed. I found a fresh lock on a door, with evidence of recent activity. That particular tunnel leads to a nearby ravine where some small vessels are moored."

Yardley stood up and pounded his fist on the desk. "This is becoming personal," he growled. "We should commence searching at once."

"Not so fast," David cautioned. "It is likely someone is checking frequently, if not a full-time guard in place. I did not run into anyone tonight, but I suspect any small sign of our presence would tip them the wink. It is imperative we catch them."

"What do you propose?"

"I think we need to search methodically, both on land and sea. Lord Wyndham, if you could arrange a search of your land along the coast, since your property begins on the other side of the ravine, that would be enormously helpful. Captain Harris, if you could organize more patrols in the water between Shoreham and Newhaven? Perhaps even a blockade, if it comes to that."

"I think that is an excellent idea," Harris agreed.

"I will request more officers for land patrols," Prescott added.

"My feeling is they are using Yardley's boat and his property for this operation as a means to deflect any blame. I suspect those old tunnels are one of their hiding places, with their convenience to the ravine. The question is, how do we access them without alerting the enemy?"

Cavenray, who had been listening with an expression of intense concentration, spoke up. "Do we need to remove the women and children? After last time, when Lord and Lady Brennan were shot, I would prefer our families be far away."

"We can move everyone to the Court," Lord Wyndham offered. "The funeral is over and there is plenty of room."

"Charlotte is the only one living here now, so if it appears the guests are all leaving, it will probably make the smugglers less wary—if they even know we are here," Yardley remarked.

"I assure you, they are aware," David responded. "Brennan had spies in places you would never imagine. When Cavenray arrived last summer, Brennan grew anxious and began making mistakes."

"Do we not want them to make mistakes?" Wyndham asked.

"Yes, but not at the cost of lives," Cavenray answered.

"This location has been ideal because my mother and sister were not exactly *watchful*. All of us arriving en masse has likely caused some paranoia amongst the gang's leadership."

"And while most free-traders are not violent, often the leaders will do anything to protect their operations and, possibly, a man prominent in Society. This type of shipment could be lucrative enough to allow a man financial freedom," David said.

"If it looks as though we are all leaving, will they relax their guard?" Yardley asked.

"I would assume so," David answered.

"Then we shall make it appear so."

"I would like to search the library for any signs of the old tunnel entrance." David rose to go and search.

"Be my guest. Jeffries might remember."

CHAPTER 12

Never again will I read a Gothic suspense...—15 Feb

*D*o not think about the mice. Do not think about the mice," Charlotte commanded herself through chattering teeth. "What would one of your heroines do? A source of light would magically appear or her hero would come to the rescue," she answered dryly in her one-sided conversation.

Reality being what it was, there was no light. She eased as close as she dared to the wall, hoping to hear signs of human life on the other side. There was nothing but silence. "Where will the family be now? The women will be in the drawing room and the men are, no doubt, still in the study, talking about breeding and brandy."

Taking the poker, she began to tap on the wall. Perhaps, if fortune favoured her, she would strike the latch and this nightmare would be over with the swirl of the fireplace.

Tap, tap, tap, tap, tap. She began to tap the beats to her favourite country jig to calm herself and keep her mind away from rodents.

When that ended, she began a vocal rendition of *Bluebells of Scotland* and her voice sent an eerie echo through the tunnels. If that did not bring someone running, what would? Of course, she had to change the words to fit the man of her dreams:

OH WHERE, tell me, where is your pirate laddie gone?
  Oh where, tell me, where is your pirate laddie gone?
  He's gone with teams of smugglers where ignoble deeds are done
  And my sad heart will tremble till he comes safely home.
  Oh where, tell me, where did your pirate laddie stay?
  Oh where, tell me, where did your pirate laddie stay?
  He dwelt beneath the moon and stars beside the crashing sea
  Where your heart followed him the night he went away.
  He dwelt beneath the moon and stars beside the crashing sea
  And many a heartache followed him the night he went away.

THEN, becoming desperate as the cold seeped into her bones, she started pleading with the wall to move.

"What have I ever done to you? Other than burn lovely warm fires inside you? Indeed, it would be rather sporting of you to be lit at the moment," she chastised the inanimate object. "I would have light and could stay warm. 'Tis too much to ask,' did I hear you say?"

"Is someone there?" She heard a muffled voice through the wall. She could not make out to whom it belonged.

"Yes! Yes! Help!" she shouted, putting her ear closer to hear better.

"Lady Charlotte? How did you get behind the wall?"

"I hit the sconce on the wall by accident. It broke and the fireplace spun around. Please get me out of here!"

"I am trying to do so. Stay calm," he said.

"It is dark and there are mice! I am not sure calm is possible!" she replied frantically.

"I am looking for the device which opens the door. There is no sconce on this side."

"And I am afraid I broke the one on my side. What do you see there?"

"A bookcase."

"Try pulling on all the books. That is how it works in novels," she said, grinning to herself at the ludicrous idea that she could be an authority on such a thing.

"Very well. This could take a while."

She heard book after book being withdrawn and dropped, presumably on the floor, and she grew impatient.

"Try the right-hand side. The latch was to the left of the fireplace, of a height with my head." She recalled the offending object easily, thanks to the bump on her head.

"Useful information," he said in a sarcastic tone. It was followed by silence.

"Where did you go? Keep talking to me! Do not leave me!"

"Hold on, my lady," she heard him say before a click pierced the heavy blackness and the wall opened. Sir David was suddenly there, jamming a chair in the opening to keep the door ajar before stepping inside to join her in the hidden room.

"Thank God!" she exclaimed as she threw her arms around him.

"You are chilled to the bone!" he said as he ran his hands up and down her bare arms.

"I thought I was going to freeze to death in here—or have a heart spasm."

"A heart spasm?" She could hear the amusement in his voice.

"Mice," she explained.

"Amongst other creatures," he agreed, the wretched man.

The warmth of his arms around her felt so very good. She could feel him trying to release her but she would not let go.

"Lady Charlotte, we must go back inside so you can warm yourself. I need to investigate this room."

"Why ever would you want to do that?"

"It was supposed to be sealed."

She could hear the prevarication in his voice.

"And?"

"And I must ensure there is no hidden access to the house."

"Does this have to do with smuggling?"

He hesitated.

"Yardley told me," she prompted, hoping he would not ask her to say more.

"Come inside. I will fetch a lantern."

They stepped back through the narrow opening and she sat on the sofa with relief, revelling in the warmth and light. Sir David left the room and returned with a lantern and two cloaks. He wrapped one around her and she snuggled into it.

"Shall I call for your maid?" he asked as he once more stepped away from her.

"Are you not going to explain?" she returned, unable to hide her disappointment.

"I must have a look around before I can answer."

"Then I shall wait."

He scowled, much like her brother did when he was displeased. Unlike her brother, he seemed to swallow his spleen and walked over to pour a glass of brandy. He returned to her and handed her the glass before picking up the lantern and returning through the secret panel.

Charlotte wrinkled her nose at the brandy. It smelled rather like the turpentine used to clean paintbrushes. She did not care for spirits of any kind, but she supposed a sip or two might help her stop shivering. With each sip, her body began to warm and relax. She dearly wanted to know what Sir David was unearthing in that room—but not quite enough to go back in there. Curiosity killed the cat, after all.

Nevertheless, growing impatient, she did rise and light a taper, in order to look through the opening. Holding her candle up high, she brought her other hand to her mouth. The flickering flame illuminated a cave-like room the size of a small ballroom. Wooden crates were stacked from floor to ceiling, almost filling the entire room. She gasped. "What is all of this?"

She heard David's footsteps approach and then he appeared around one of the stacks.

"Something you would be better not to know," he replied.

"Then I shall look for myself," she said haughtily, stepping back into the cave. It was not so scary with light... except that, tipsy from the spirits, she tripped and knocked the chair back. The door slammed behind them, blowing her taper out.

Sir David let out an oath as he caught her in his arms.

She began to giggle.

"No more spirits for you, ever."

"It is quite humorous."

"Except for the fact that the latch is broken from this side," he pointed out.

"Oh. Oh no!"

The door at the other end of the room began to rattle.

"Hush!" he whispered into her ear, drawing her down behind a crate and turning down his light. "They will not hesitate to slit your throat and leave you to the rodents," he warned.

She swallowed hard and hoped they could not hear her heart pounding.

"I DO NOT THINK we should be here with all them swells visiting."

"Well, *all them swells* are starting to sniff around. Deuced bad luck them arriving just now. One house party could undo months of work!"

"They think this room is sealed."

"Let us not give them a reason to suspect otherwise. Is all of it here?"

"Except for the ammunition, yessir. We just got to finish this last run and will be in the clear."

"Then see it done as quickly as possible. We must make certain this run happens without incident. Dispose of anyone who gets in the way."

FOOTSTEPS ECHOED as they walked toward the door and left. The lock clicked and the key turned. Charlotte was too scared to move. She could feel David's breath on her neck and a thrill of awareness caused her to tremble. It was a strange mixture of fear and anticipation. They stayed there, his arms still holding her safe, for a few more minutes. Growing impatient, she wriggled around to face him.

"Be still, woman! You will be the death of me yet," he muttered.

She looked up. "What is going on? Who were those men?"

David sighed.

"First, let me determine if we can get out of here without alarming the whole household. Then I shall endeavour to explain as much as I can."

He attempted to step back but she held on.

"Will that explanation include why you insist on rejecting me?" Where had this boldness come from? It was much easier in the dark—and with the false courage of brandy.

"I have already explained."

"Very unsatisfactorily, too, if I might say so. I know there is a kind, honourable side to you," she taunted.

"What else is there to say, Lady Charlotte?" he asked. Kneeling down, he relit the lantern before regaining his feet to pierce her with those grey, grey eyes. "Stop trying to make a hero out of me. I will never be what you deserve or want."

"Then be a rogue and kiss me." She stepped closer, tempting fate. He stood as still as marble, watching her. A dark lock fell over his forehead, making him look more tempting. Reaching up, she stroked his cheek and then his beard.

His breath hitched and she grew bolder.

"Lady Charlotte, this is very ill-advised."

"For whom? Do I repulse you?"

He swallowed hard and gave a slight shake of his head. "Of course not."

"Then what is wrong with a simple kiss?"

"There is nothing simple about it, my lady."

She stood on her tiptoes and brushed her lips across his.

"Nothing can come of this. Of us," he said, in little more than a whisper.

"Why not?" she asked. She slid her arms around his neck and boldly kissed him with all the years of pent up longing she held in her heart. Perhaps it would convince him she was in earnest. How could he be so wrong for her when he was the first man ever to feel right? She knew the moment he stopped resisting and kissed her back. It was every bit as wonderful as she remembered from her dreams, and more. He smelled of spice and tasted of brandy, the fire of both coursed through her body. His whiskers were rough in contrast to the warm silkiness of his lips, which caressed and devoured. For a moment, she could not think as her mind swirled with sensations.

It was not long enough before the latch clicked and they spun about to face a room full of shocked faces.

***

There were guests and servants standing in the opening, staring at them. David could only imagine what they were thinking. Lady Charlotte was dirty, dishevelled and looking thoroughly kissed, thanks to his scratchy beard.

Yardley looked about to have an apoplectic fit. David had broken his word. The Lord knew he had tried to be honourable, but Lady Charlotte had turned into a vixen no flesh and bone man could have resisted. Wellington could have used her skill to torture their prisoners!

"Everyone out," Yardley growled.

As the onlookers obeyed, except for the Duchess, the Duke continued to stand with his arms folded, looking furious.

David remained quiet, not thinking explanations would help at this point. Of course, he would marry Lady Charlotte if necessary, but he did not think, even in such a situation, that the Duke would welcome such a lowly alliance.

"You might as well come out," he growled. "You cannot hide in there forever."

David handed Charlotte into the room and she took up an offensive stance against her brother immediately. "It is not what you think, Benedict."

"Regardless of what I may or may not *think*, I saw you in each other's embrace."

"He rescued me! I was merely showing him my gratitude."

David swallowed a chuckle and took a sudden interest in his boots.

Yardley kept his eyes narrowed, as though trying to compose himself. His wife's hand was on his arm, as if warning him.

"Do you not consider, Sir David, this would be the appropriate time to state your intentions towards Lady Charlotte?" the Duchess suggested.

"Not now, Jolie," Yardley commanded. "At least Prescott and Davenport have left."

"I do not think any such declaration would be welcome or accepted by your husband, your Grace—even if Lady Charlotte were to accept. I am too far beneath her touch not to be considered guilty of lowering her reputation further."

"Enough! We can discuss my reputation later. There are more important matters, are there not, Sir David?" Charlotte looked to him to explain.

"Indeed. Lady Charlotte has stumbled upon what we were looking for. Behind this wall is a room full of guns."

"Behind this wall?" the Duchess asked.

"How did you find it? Why were you even searching?" Yardley asked his sister.

"It was pure accident," she confessed. "I broke the sconce on the wall, and the fireplace turned beneath my feet. I had no light or way to escape." She shuddered visibly.

"I came in here to seek this very thing," David said, "when I heard her singing behind the wall. She told me where to look and I began removing books until I found the right one."

"That much I surmised. It is how we knew where to look," Yardley replied dryly. He indicated the pile of books and overturned chair. "Did you not have the sense not to repeat her mistake?"

Lady Charlotte spoke. "That was my fault. He lodged a chair to hold the wall open, but I tripped over it and locked us in again. Then we heard people trying to break into the tunnel, talking about disposing of anyone who got in their way, and I quite lost my mind," she rambled.

The Duchess hurried over and took Charlotte in her arms. "You poor dear. How afraid you must have been! Should we send someone after the intruders, Benedict?"

"Why do you not see her to her chamber while I hear the rest of the story? We will send someone if need be," Yardley said to his wife. The ladies retreated, though Lady Charlotte gave a warning glare to her brother that almost made David laugh aloud. He did not, however, for the Duke cleared his throat in an ominous fashion.

"Would you rather tell me or show me what is behind that wall? And, more importantly, who were the men who have been using my name and property, seeming at their leisure, to arm our enemies?"

David gestured with his hands towards a pair of armchairs. "I think discussion is our better course at this juncture." He knew Yardley's ire was genuine. Any doubts he had about his involvement were gone. "With your sister present, I did not dare attempt to look. Dunn was one of them. The other sounded like a gentleman, whose voice I did not recognize."

"So, it is possible the gentleman was Reverend Howard?"

"It is."

"Were you able to overhear anything useful?"

"Not as much as I would have liked, though they did confirm that all of the arms are stored here and the ammunition is not."

In evident frustration, Yardley ran his hands over his face and through his hair. "What do you suggest we do?"

"Moving the arms would most likely cause us to lose the bigger prize and not stop the operation—only suspend it."

"I agree. And I want to know who the wretch is that dares attempt to blacken my name for his purposes."

"Brennan would have dared. However, I think this is more a matter of convenience."

"Using my yacht?" Yardley elevated an eyebrow in question. "Using my land?"

"Perhaps. Do you have any enemies, your Grace?

"I thought they were buried with my former wife. I have no controversial bills up before the Lords. No, I cannot think of anyone who would attempt to implicate me in this."

"Then I suggest we remove the ladies as planned and continue to search. I would station guards discreetly, to keep an eye on the arms in case the plan changes or someone warns them off."

"Do you think there is a spy in my household?"

"Most likely, or else they would not be so bold as to use your property. Your arrival was a surprise."

"Very well. I will organize the posting of the guards personally, using my footmen from London who have no suspicion attached, nor reason to snitch against me."

"A wise choice, your Grace. I would also keep our plans to ourselves. Only tell each person as little as necessary."

"Now, what are we do to about my sister?"

CHAPTER 13

Guilt is always a winning tactic when you cannot get your way in a respectable fashion.—16 Feb

The next morning, Charlotte woke to a flurry of activity amongst the household. Servants were rushing to and fro beyond her door, accompanied by the rattle of trunks being carried downstairs, and the sounds of domestic upheaval echoed through the halls.

"What is going on, Chapman?" Charlotte asked when her maid brought in her morning chocolate. Following the adventure, Charlotte had been awake rather late, and she was not appreciative of early morning on a good day.

"The Duchess and Lady Wyndham have taken a notion into their heads about presenting Miss Letty to the *ton*. If that were not enough, they have decided they must all remove to Wyndham to plan it," Chapman grumbled, having more freedom of speech than an average lady's maid, since she had been Charlotte's nursery maid.

Charlotte dressed and made her way down to the chaos. Servants were moving trunks, and every carriage and cart was being loaded for the mass exodus. She hoped they did not expect her to participate in this when for once there was so much excitement to be had at home.

"I suspect that is what this is all about. They want the ladies out of the way in case there is danger," she said to herself. "Well, they had better not try to force me to leave my home."

Deciding to stake her claim from the beginning, she sought out Yardley in his study.

"Good morning, Lottie." he brother greeted her, rising when she entered before returning to his seat. "You do not look any the worse for wear. I did not have a chance to ensure you were all right last night."

"I was shaken, but Sir David helped me keep my wits." *With the help of brandy*, she added silently, but she would omit that detail. "Now, I would like to know what is going on. The whole truth, if you please."

Her brother narrowed his gaze and began stroking his chin as he was wont to do when he was contemplating something distasteful.

She took a seat, revelling in his discomfort. She could wait him out.

"Very well, what would you like to know?"

"Besides why you lied to me, you mean? You did not hurt him or call him out, did you?"

"I have not determined how to solve that problem, yet. We must first deal with the smuggling situation." He stood and walked around his desk to join her.

"Is that why there is a room full of guns in the tunnel?"

"Yes, and Douglas was sent here to expose the leader."

"I knew it! I knew there was more to this than Sir David being a servant!"

"That is confidential information, Charlotte. His identity must remain concealed or it could compromise the entire undertaking. I have only told you in order to make you see reason, to keep you safe."

"Regardless of that, I am eight-and-twenty, dear brother, and I do not intend to remove to Wyndham."

"Charlotte," he growled.

"This is my home. I have never removed to Wyndham. Do you not think that would alert the gang more than my staying here?"

"That is a risk I am willing to take. Your life is worth more to me than catching the smugglers. There will be other chances, I am sure."

"Not for me. And what of Sir David?"

"He is not my primary concern."

"What if he is pardoned?"

"He will still have a criminal past, Charlotte."

"Yet if it matters not to me? You have had your chance at happiness, Brother. He is the first man to make me feel like…like I am worthy."

"How will you feel should you be shunned in Society? If your children are ridiculed and the centre of jests?"

"We could live at his plantation."

Yardley shook his head. "You have not thought about this in a detached manner. You are thinking with emotion, not your head. And what does Douglas say to this? Have the two of you already planned what lies ahead?"

"No," she hung her head. "He will not even discuss a future with me."

"Then he is wiser than I gave him credit for." His eyebrows lifted in obvious pleasant surprise.

"I know he cares for me, Benedict. He makes me feel special, cared about."

"You do not need a man to make you feel special, Charlotte—and you must know you are cared about!" He stepped closer and wrapped his arms around her.

"My mind knows that, but my heart feels indescribable when I am with him. I intend to fight for him if necessary, Benedict. I would much prefer your support than to have to battle you as well. We have enough against us as it is."

There was a slight knock on the door. Jolie's beautiful face peered around the panel. "May I intrude?"

"Of course." Benedict answered before he committed himself to Charlotte, she could not help but notice. He kissed his wife on the cheek and Charlotte tried not to be jealous. She was happy for them, truly; she just wanted that for herself, too.

"Is everything packed and ready for departure?"

"Almost. Lady Brennan and Letty have already taken their leave. I was waiting to accompany Charlotte."

"I am not going," she said firmly.

"But you must!" Jolie exclaimed. "Do you not wish to be a part of Letty's come out?"

"Of course I wish to support her, but you, Elly and her mother do not need my help. The three of you could run the War Office."

Her brother snorted and covered it with a cough.

"Benedict, you must make her go. It is not safe for her to stay here!"

"I am sorry, my dearest, but she wishes to stay. She thinks it will raise more suspicion if she leaves."

"Charlotte, do you really think so?" Jolie pleaded.

"I do. I could come for the day and return in the evening, as I normally do. Would that suffice?"

"I will still be here with her at night," Benedict assured his wife, "though we intend to keep the fact mum. Davenport and Prescott will stay in the cottages."

"So everyone will think you have left?" Charlotte asked.

"That is my intention. I do not even want the household to know, other than my servants from London."

"Do you think there is a tattler in the household?" she asked with surprise.

"Douglas does. It may not even be intentional, but small things, like an order from the butcher, give away the fact that the family is in residence. Unfortunately, there is always someone willing to talk for enough coin."

"I suppose so. Hopefully this will be over with quickly and everything can go back to normal."

"Yes, normal," Charlotte echoed, her features composed. Deep in her heart, she hoped fervently for so much more.

DESPITE SEARCHING all day for where the ammunition was hidden, they found nothing. David was now on his way to participate in his first smuggling run with the gang, and the others were meeting at Wyndham for dinner. He could only hope that someone would let something slip tonight, though he never would have been so careless as a leader.

Lord willing, this would be his penultimate run as a smuggler. Pretending to be someone you were not was so very exhausting, yet it was the price he must pay for the jealousy and greed of his youth.

He dressed in black trousers, shirt and boots and placed his black cap on his head. His dark beard hid his face well enough that he did not need to darken his skin with soot.

As he made his way through the dense fog to the meeting point near the village, he thought about his exchanges with Prescott, Harris and Davenport earlier in the day. Could they be trusted? Yardley seemed to have faith in them, but David had learned early in his career that few men had the honour they proclaimed, especially when it came to women, finances and pride. Regardless of his misgivings, they had searched by his side all day, to no avail. Wyndham had had no success either. Extra soldiers were to arrive soon and ships were to be put in place, yet he kept having this nagging feeling the smugglers would move the goods early. Yardley arriving with his entourage had frightened the gentleman leading this. It was beginning to feel eerily like Brennan's downfall. He had to tread very carefully to make sure it was not his.

"Douglas," Captain Dunn greeted him as the workers met at the rendezvous point near the Saltdean Gap. "I heard word all of the guests have departed from Langborn."

"Aye. You know how the nobility is. The Duchess had a whim to go somewhere and the Duke indulged it." He spat with disgust.

Dunn eyed him with obvious approval. "I, for one, am glad for their whims. I never did like them sniffing around. Ye never know when they might take a fancy to act all righteous, as if they don't know where their fine tea and brandy comes from."

David grunted his agreement. The less said the better.

A young man swaggered into the tunnel with his chest puffed out, full of his own consequence.

"What has ye lookin' like a cock in a hen house, Clifford?" Dunn asked, grinning, revealing crooked, yellowed teeth.

"Let me jus' say, Nibley will spend his evenin' on a wild goose chase."

"Is that so? Well, tell me, what have ye done?"

"I rearranged all his purty little trail markers, is what I done. He'll be in Brighton afore he realizes." The young man guffawed, along with most of the fifty or so men gathered, all dressed in black with darkened faces.

"The fog won't hurt his confusion, either," Dunn added. "Time to go." The leader began dividing up the labour, some to row, some to climb.

Since he had a horse, David was assigned to keep watch from the eastern side. The Reverend Howard was the western lookout, closer to the village, as usual. Once all the goods were unloaded and in the tunnels, it would be transported to the church.

A light flashed out on the water, and at the signal the men set out to meet the incoming ship. At the sound of the oars slicing through the water, David set Gulliver to the chalk cliffs, climbing eastward, shrouded in the mist. It was a perfect night for the trade, with visibility low. Even if you could hear, you could not see more than twenty feet in front of you. There would not be much warning if the Revenue came upon them. He cocked his gun and placed it in his waist-band, then strained his eyes to see and his ears to hear. The biting wind was fierce up on the cliffs, an unwelcome addition to an already distasteful undertaking. Fleetingly, his thoughts strayed to Lady Charlotte, all warm and tucked up in her bed—and wishing he might join her—before he dismissed them as pointless.

Walking on, alone with his thoughts, he realized it was a decided disadvantage to be a stranger to these lands. Back home in Westmorland, he had known every rock and crevice to avoid. In the fog, it was slow going to make sure he and Gulliver avoided the cliff's edge and stayed aware of how far they had walked. It could have been half a mile or more already, but if he went too far back from the edge, he would possibly miss any ships coming in from the east. Gulliver's ears flattened before David heard the cry for help. He looked forward and saw what appeared to be someone falling over the cliff's edge. Dismounting as far back from the edge as he could reasonably do for his mount's safety, and telling Gulliver to stand, he ran forward on foot.

He was too late. Dunn was there before him, kicking loose the fingers with which Officer Nibley had been barely hanging on.

The sickening thud he heard, as the Revenue man landed on the rocks below, would haunt David for his lifetime. It was low tide, and there was no soft reprieve for the poor Exciseman's body. Dunn did not even look to see what became of the man, as he marched on towards the east. It did not appear he had noticed David, either.

Where was he off to? The run was happening in the other direction! Feeling torn, David peered over the edge to see if there was any chance of saving Nibley. He could not make out the body clearly through the dense sky, but he knew there was almost no chance of surviving that fall.

Reluctantly, he felt as though he must follow Dunn. He returned to Gulliver, not wishing his horse to suffer the same fate as the Revenue man, but there was nowhere to tether him here with only tall grass covering the cliff. He led the horse, creeping along at a snail's pace, not wanting to overtake Dunn, when the sounds of digging echoed from the beach below, the occasional strike of shovel against stone sharp in the misty atmosphere. He had been sent on a diversion run! He muttered oaths under his breath. There was no way to alert Yardley and the rest at this point.

Once again, David left Gulliver as far back from the edge as possible and crept forward to the edge to see, hiding as best he could in tussocks and tall grass.

At least twenty men were scaling up and down the cliffs on ropes, carrying sacks. More men were down on the beach. The tide was out and they were digging near the cliff face, burying the goods as they were brought down.

David breathed a small sigh of relief. At least the goods were not being sent out that night, although it begged the questions, when would they be and what would happen now? Should he return to the other run so he did not alert Dunn? He could always claim Gulliver had stumbled and gone lame. The thought of Lady Charlotte, all alone at the house while the smugglers were removing goods, made him uneasy. Would she hear them and feel compelled to do something? There really was no choice to be had. He must go and ensure she was safe.

CHAPTER 14

Why is danger so tempting? The more I attempt to reason with myself to stay away, the more I decide I must dive head first into it. After all, what have I to lose?—17 Feb

Charlotte could sense that something was wrong the moment she returned to Langborn from spending the day at Wyndham. She had left her brother at the empty gardener's cottage and come back to the house alone. It was eerily quiet when she set foot in the house and immediately she felt unnerved.

Had Yardley given everyone the evening off without telling her? It was something he would do, but why? Was it part of the ruse to make the gang leader more comfortable; to entice him into a trap? Walking through the house, there was not a servant to be found. Was the entire household involved in smuggling and she had never noticed?

The kitchens were empty, as was the housekeeper's room. Charlotte knew her brother was not far away, but could not help wondering when he would join her. If he had given all the servants the night off, why was he waiting to return to the house?

Tiptoeing back up the stairs, Charlotte went to the library. If something was going forward, she might be able to hear through the wall. Should she go and fetch her brother and David? It had been easy to be brave when she thought the house full of servants, but there was definitely something amiss. She took a small pistol from the desk. Recalling how she had laughed at her brother when he had given it to her, now she was grateful—even though she hoped it would not be necessary to use it. There was also a small folding knife in the drawer and she hesitated with her hand above it. In sudden decision, she grabbed hold of it and put it into the pocket of her cloak. Were not the heroines always prepared in her books? She snorted to herself at the thought of being able to do anything which could be considered heroic. However, something was happening; something which might involve Sir David, and if she could, she had to help.

Placing her ear against the fireplace, while being careful not to have a repeat of revolving into a cave, she strained for any signs of activity. Hearing none, she desperately wished she knew whereabouts the other door led out. Should she go in search of it alone? No, that would be foolish in the extreme. The wise thing would be to find her brother. Where was he? He had said he would join her here shortly.

She jumped as a crash sounded on the other side of the fireplace. In that moment, everything became real. She was alone in this house and beyond the secret door there were dangerous men who would kill her. If only she had a servant to send for Yardley! It would take too long to run to the stables.

What should she do? There was little she *could* do in these frivolous skirts and slippers. She made a swift decision to change into something warmer and more practical before leaving via the kitchens to see what she could find. Perhaps it was simply large rats overturning something that had caused the sound. Unfortunately, she could not convince herself.

Pulling her hood up over her head, she stepped out into the cold and dark. She did not dare carry a lantern for fear of being detected. How many times had she been out here by day? But nothing was the same at night. The bushes seemed to have doubled in size. The trees had become bandits lying in wait. Owls hooting beyond the kitchen garden were ravaging beasts. Her boots, crunching in the frozen grass, sounded like the fireworks at Vauxhall. If there was anyone standing watch, they would be certain to hear her coming.

Her main problem was that she did not know where the entrance to the tunnel was located. What would she do if she found someone? Halting in her tracks, she began to reconsider her hasty dive into detection... but what if she saw or overheard something that would allow Sir David to be pardoned?

Stepping slowly forward through the garden as she considered, the decision was made for her. A man was entering a wooden service door behind the conservatory and she followed him. Was it Sir David? It was too dark to make out any features, but he was tall like him. If she could, she had to help him.

Charlotte waited a few minutes and then slipped through the door in the man's wake. The dirty, musty scent of the damp underground assailed her nose. Immediately, there was a set of steps leading downward into the earth. She eased the door slowly closed behind her before stopping to allow her eyes to adjust.

"Perhaps it is not the wisest choice to enter a dark room without a lantern," she muttered dryly, pulling her cloak tighter as she lowered her foot slowly, one step and then the next. "Did I learn nothing from last time?" On this occasion not to be deterred by thoughts of spiders and rodents, she stepped gingerly, one foot in front of the other, feeling more and more like a coward than one of her heroines. She had to remind herself sternly that she had survived the previous night's excursion in order to keep from running back to the house. She still did not know what would happen when she arrived. She had no clear idea of what the room at the end looked like, and she was hoping she could hide once she reached the storage chamber. At least the passage was tall and wide enough that she need not touch the sides.

As she drew closer, she could hear sounds; not the sounds of voices but of work being done—footsteps, wheels turning and, perhaps, crates being opened and moved.

Should she turn around and go to find her brother? What if she was too late, by that point, to discover who the culprit was? Perhaps if she went a little bit further, she might see something useful.

There was light at the end of the tunnel when she drew closer. Careful to remain in the shadows, she followed, finding a support beam behind which she could conceal herself. She had to swallow a gasp as a man came within two feet of her, and then another. They were dressed all in black with dark caps and soot covering their faces. They were entering a room and coming out again carrying large, white oilcloth bags that strained with the weight of their load. Where could they be going?

She followed on behind the light from their lantern—as close as she dared—when she heard their footsteps recede. They came to another tunnel which went in a different direction, but where did it lead? To the cliffs and the sea? Of course, it must do so, for where else would they be going? She had to follow them and then get the information to Benedict. It was the only way she could envisage any kind of future with Sir David.

Her heart hammered with fright, so loudly she feared it would give her presence away. Inhaling two deep breaths, she then followed, clinging to the sides, praying she would not be discovered. Sounds of water dripping began to grow louder as a breeze and the smell of sea air grew stronger. Pausing to still her shaking knees, which she was struggling to control, she willed herself to be calm.

Her heart in her mouth, she crept the final steps to the outside, peering around the edge; this was the moment of truth. Would there be anything beyond the mouth of the cave?

She took a sideways step and strained to see. It was pitch black at first, although, as her eyes adjusted, she saw a small reflection against the white cliffs. Looking up, it appeared she was in a ravine. Was this the same ravine she jumped so often at its narrowest point? Where had the men gone? Were they lying in wait to grab her?

The tide was out, and she stepped down a rock-strewn slope on to the beach, taking care to hold on to the cliff face so as not to slip and be discovered. There was still no sign of the smugglers, so she ventured further and looked around a promontory of the cliffs. Were they already gone? Had she been too late?

Scrambling along the face, she found a deeply shadowed crevice to hide in. Straining her eyes to see in the darkness, she finally glimpsed men digging in the sand where the tide had receded from the beach. They were burying the bags they had carried out of the store-room. She heard the scuffle of feet just short of her hiding place and had to smother an involuntary squeak. Two voices began to speak. Although her body was shaking with terror, she strived to listen to the conversation.

"WE ARE ALMOST FINISHED, sir. This will be a sweet reward."

"Indeed. It will revolutionize warfare. To think of self-contained cartridges fashioned from paper."

"Stuff it down the barrel, put on a new percussion cap and it's ready to fire," the other man added with excitement.

"And it is all safe on the ship?"

"Aye, sir. We will come back for the munitions on the next low tide."

"The cartridges are the most urgent business for now. It is better to be cautious with the rest."

DECIDING she had seen and heard enough, Charlotte began to back away towards the ravine and relative safety. Without warning, an arm came around her neck.

"Stop right there, my lady." She knew that voice.

"Let me go!" she commanded, struggling to wrench free of the arm encircling her. Clutching wildly, she managed to rip his neckcloth.

"I am afraid you have seen too much. You should have stayed abed, like good ladies do," he growled in her ear.

"What are you going to do with me?" She swallowed hard.

"Make your death appear an unfortunate accident."

He could not mean it! She twisted in an attempt to break free of his grasp. His arm tightened and tortured gasps of air gagged her. Desperation aiding her dwindling courage, she bit his restraining hand and her anguished cry for help rent through the air.

ONCE DAVID HAD DECIDED he needed to ensure Charlotte's safety, he began to feel urgent—almost frantic. By the time he reached the house, it was shrouded in darkness and the front door was locked. Was he worrying for nothing? Were they all abed and none the wiser of the criminal activity taking place beneath their noses?

He walked stealthily around to the servant's entrance, just to satisfy himself. The door was open and he found the kitchens were dark. Something was off, but it did not mean anything untoward had happened. He lit a taper and crept up the back stairs just to see if he could determine if Lady Charlotte was safely tucked in her bed, but when he reached the family apartments, all of the doors were opened and the rooms empty. He rushed down the main stairs and into the library. Silence. Darkness. He ran back down to the kitchens and knocked on the housekeeper's door. When there was no answer, he flung it open to discover the room was also empty. There was no one in the house!

Rushing back to the stables, he roused everyone and sent a groom to fetch Yardley from the gardener's cottage. Why had he not suspected they would move sooner? Where was Lady Charlotte? He would forfeit his pardon and everything he owned to ensure her safety. He should have insisted that Yardley send everyone to London!

He took a lantern and ran to the tunnel entrance. The door was unlocked. It did not mean that Charlotte was in there, of course. He pressed forward blindly; his presence could be explained away. He stopped at the door leading to the entrance of the storage chamber behind the library and the lock was undone. He pulled open the door and held his lantern high, scanning the vault for any sign of Charlotte or the smugglers. The room was empty. They had moved quickly.

Muttering an oath of frustration, he began to move through the chamber. Then he heard what sounded like a cry for help. He lifted the lantern and scanned the room again. In the far corner, he found several people tied up and gagged. He took out his knife and released each of Langborn's servants, one by one.

"Where is Lady Charlotte? Have they taken her somewhere?"

"We don't rightly know, sir. She was not home when they came in and took us."

"Is there a chance she stayed at Wyndham?"

"We don't know that either, sir," the old butler answered, clearly shaken.

"Everyone go back inside the house and warm yourselves. Be prepared for anything. I sent one of the grooms for the Duke. When he arrives, tell him I am going through the tunnel into the ravine, looking for Lady Charlotte."

With having lost precious moments, David hurried through the passageway, hoping and praying that Lady Charlotte had stayed at Wyndham Court. Something inside told him they were not so fortunate.

As he reached the opening to the ravine and crept towards the beach, he looked down as cold water began to pour over his boots. The tide was coming back in! Heedless of the loose footing, he ran down the slope to the beach, only to catch a glimpse of the workers loading up the rowing boats he had seen earlier. Where could she be? His eyes searched furiously, trying to discern if there was a lady amongst the men. What would he do in this situation if he were Captain Dunn? He would never have bothered the people in the house.

What an ugly thought to have. He never could have harmed a lady, no matter how dire the circumstances. But Dunn was cut from a different cloth and he suspected they would hesitate no more than a moment because she was the sister of a Duke. They would try to make her murder look like an accident.

"In all probability she is tucked up in a warm, comfortable bed at Wyndham," he muttered, trying to reassure himself.

"But what if Dunn has her?" He could not wait here to find out. He lifted his gaze and squinted through the swirling fog, with a growing sense of desperation. Some of the boats were already on their way out into deeper waters, the men bent to the oars and the hulls slipping back and forth through the waves.

That was when he saw her struggling against someone. Only fifteen yards ahead, the water was rising and it appeared she was being dragged out farther. She would be no match for any of them—if the waves or her heavy skirts did not carry her under first.

David pulled his gun out and kept moving forward, the waves lapping at his boots as he wound around the rocky outcrops of the cliffs. He was still too far to take a shot without risking hitting Lady Charlotte. He lost them for a moment as a patch of fog floated by and he focused his gaze and strained his ears to find them.

"Ouch, you little witch!" The man yelped. She must have kicked his shin.

"Good girl, keep fighting," David mumbled to himself as he crept closer through the water. The tide was rushing in quickly; it already reached his knees...

The man tried to push her under the water and David could not wait any longer to act.

A yacht had crept in through the fog, and someone yelled. "Hurry, sir! *The Nelson* is coming in from the east!"

David would swear that was Dunn calling from the boat. So who had Charlotte?

Making an instant decision, David acted. "Let her go! Do you really want the Duke to be after you?"

"It is too late for that. She has seen everything!" David recognized the voice but could not place it. It was definitely a gentleman, not Dunn.

"What do you mean to do with her?" David called. He hoped that with every moment he delayed, he would have a better chance of saving her. By voicing it out loud, he hoped that the man would reconsider hurting Charlotte.

David crouched down into the water, aiming his gun. The yacht was creeping closer, though if it came too much further in, it would run aground.

"Stop fighting me!" the man commanded.

"Never!" she shouted.

"Come now, sir, or I'll have to leave ye," Dunn called from the ship.

The man turned a fraction and began to drag Charlotte towards the boat.

David's finger pulled on the trigger. The man released his hold on Charlotte just as she fired a shot herself. The man fell back into the water but David's only thought was for Charlotte. Without the man holding her, the water would saturate her skirts and pull her down to a watery grave.

As David ran to help her, the sounds of gunfire began to pop off like fireworks. Suddenly, the yacht ignited into a giant fireball. He took the gun from Charlotte's hands, which she was still pointing at the ship. Her shaking body came willingly into his arms; lifting her, he trudged against the water towards the shore.

"What on earth is happening?" Yardley's voice boomed over the noise seconds before he and Davenport appeared out of the fog and waded furiously into the water to help.

"Prescott!" Charlotte managed to shout through ragged breaths. "Retrieve him!" She lifted a shaking arm and pointed to a body floating face down in the swirling waters. It was starting to drift out to sea.

Davenport and Yardley set off in the other direction through the water while David continued to hold a shivering Charlotte. Before them, at no great distance, *The Jolie* went down in a cracking, hissing, wall of flames. The girl in his arms shuddered and clutched at his shoulders. Her teeth were chattering and he held her as tight as he could.

"Let me take you back to the house," David said.

"N-N-N-No." She shook her head. "Want to wait."

They watched in silence as the scene played out. It was a few more minutes before Yardley and Davenport returned, dragging Prescott's body with them.

"It looks like we found the ammunition," Yardley remarked, with a sad look at his yacht burning to embers.

"And our traitor," David replied with a disgusted scowl at Prescott's body.

CHAPTER 15

Suddenly, smelling salts make so much sense. Would that I could waft some-thing under the nose of a criminal and render him senseless.—18 Feb

*C*harlotte had never been one to simper or be silly. So why was she so hysterical? When they finally made it back to the tunnel and were out of the water, David placed her on her feet. Her knees became weak and she almost swooned. If not for Sir David, she might have fallen. Before she realized what was happening, he swooped down and gathered her into his arms and began the quickest route back to the house through the tunnels while Yardley and Davenport dealt with Prescott's body.

That snapped her out of her despondency. She was no make-weight and was very conscious of it.

"You do not need to carry me! It was just a momentary lapse, I assure you," she proclaimed.

"Nonsense. It is perfectly reasonable for you to be overset. You had to fight for your life for several minutes and you had not one, but two, opponents," he said easily, not even breathing hard.

"Two?" She tried to converse with him in a logical fashion, but speech was almost beyond her at the moment as she attempted to assimilate what had happened, along with the delightful sensation of being in David's arms.

"Prescott and the water. 'Tis very likely your skirts would have taken you under had he not been holding on to you," he explained.

"They were heavy but I had no notion of that. Thank you for saving me." She dared to look into his eyes, but the tunnels were too dark and he was staring ahead, intent on seeing their way.

"It appeared to me as though you saved yourself."

She shook her head. "No. How did you know he had caught me?"

"I did not know for certain until I saw you. I was helping with the run at the Saltdean Gap when I saw Dunn heading east—away from the action. It was then I realized I had been sent on a diversion run and I hurried back to try and warn you. I searched the house and it was completely empty."

He had been smuggling? She tried to consider that thought, but dismissed it as useless.

"That is what set me to searching. I found the servants bound and gagged and you were not with them." His voice cracked as he recalled the scene.

He had come for her! For *her*. His warm breath seared her wet skin as she shivered against him, her arms wrapped fast around his neck. They were both soaked and smelled of briny sea. Strangely, she did not find it in the least unpleasant. She snuggled closer in his arms and enjoyed the feeling of safety and protection as her nerves began to settle.

When they reached the house, a rush of warmth came over her. Sir David began issuing orders to the servants, who appeared shaken but clearly relieved to have somewhere to concentrate their nervous anxieties.

Entering the back door into the kitchen, he set her down with tenderness, as though she were a fragile, breakable object to be treated with care. For some reason, he was always making her feel special when she had never known such adoration. For a brief moment their eyes met; his were the dark grey of a winter sky and stared at her with an intense emotion that seemed to mirror her own. Suddenly, her nerves were unsettled in a wholly different manner and she felt hopeful. Their bodies were still close and, of one accord, they began to lean forward.

Then the servants bustled in with blankets and took their wet cloaks.

"Your bath is almost ready, my lady," Mrs. Huggins, the housekeeper, informed her.

"Please see that more water is readied. His Grace, Sir David and Mr. Davenport were also in the cold waters for some time." As Charlotte spoke, she recalled how all of them had suffered the freezing Channel water to save her.

"Yes, my lady." The housekeeper bobbed a curtsy and left.

"That will not be necessary, Lady Charlotte. I must be away to help tidy up the details." Sir David knelt down to help her remove her soaking, ruined boots. She was stunned at the intimacy and searched for something to say.

"Will that complete your work here?" she finally asked warily, afraid of his answer.

"I believe so, but only the King can answer that with certainty."

"I see," she said, fearing the worst. She willed her bottom lip to stop quivering. "Will you come back?"

He reached up and smoothed his thumb over her wobbling chin. The loving gesture ended her dignity completely. Never before had anyone showed her such consideration. Tears escaped the confines of her eyes and rolled down her face. "I promise you, it is better this way."

"Is arguing futile?"

"I am afraid so."

"Then this is farewell?" she asked, unwilling to believe the words he spoke.

"I cannot change my past, my lady. It will always follow me and therefore would follow you."

"I do not care!" she cried desperately, reaching for him as he began to step away.

With one final piercing look—or dare she say anguish? Or was she merely hoping his heartache mirrored her own?—he turned and left her for good.

~

LADY CHARLOTTE HAD NOT LINGERED over her bath, and was back downstairs by the time Yardley and Davenport returned. David could not look her in the eyes for it was too painful, even though he doubted she had yet seen him standing near the hearth, trying to dry his sodden boots.

The look on her face tempted him to throw reason to the wind and carry her away to the islands. Almost. However, he had promised Yardley and he also knew himself to be unworthy. The best thing he could do was remove himself from her life.

"Oh dear, Charlotte. How are you feeling? Are you dry and warm? That was quite an ordeal you met with tonight." Yardley stormed in and threw his arms around his sister.

She nodded in his embrace. "I am making shift, Brother. I thank God that Sir David arrived when he did. I do not know how much longer I could have held Prescott off."

"You have my eternal thanks, Douglas," Yardley said, turning and extending his hand.

David saw Lady Charlotte jerk when she realized he was still there. He had not expected her to leave her room that night after her harrowing ordeal. He was not certain his heart had yet settled to a normal pace.

"You almost died, Lottie." Yardley pulled back and searched his sister's eyes.

"Dying was never an option," she retorted, no doubt to reassure her brother. David had seen her fear—and her strength.

"How did you know to shoot the yacht?" Yardley asked.

"Maybe it was just a lucky shot."

"Was it?" Yardley and Charlotte exchanged bleak smiles.

"I overheard Dunn and Prescott discussing the ammunition you were looking for. They had hidden it on *The Jolie,* as you no doubt surmised," Charlotte explained. "They spoke of bullet cartridges made with paper that were self-contained. You could stuff one of these cartridges down the barrel, put on a new percussion cap and it was ready to fire. They thought to make their fortune with this new discovery."

"Indeed. It would completely transform warfare. It would take several steps out of the reloading process!"

"But why smuggle it to our enemies? Why would Prescott betray his country?" Yardley asked, disbelief and frustration displayed by his frown and his outstretched hands.

"I still cannot believe Prescott was a traitor. A man in uniform!" Davenport finally spoke.

"And one of our oldest friends," Yardley added quietly. "How did you come to be there, Charlotte?"

"Well..." She began to explain with what David was certain was a guilty look on her face. "When I returned to the house, all was dark and there was not a soul to be found."

Yardley's gaze narrowed and centred upon his sister. He crossed his arms over his chest.

"So, I decided to look and see where everyone had disappeared to. I did not think you had given the servants the night off and where would they have gone?"

"This did not cause you to think that you should come and find me?" Yardley asked, his tone derogatory.

"The thought did cross my mind, yes, but I heard a crash on the other side of the library wall and I went to investigate."

Yardley made a growling sound. "Is that when he caught you?"

"No, I actually went and changed into something warmer." Her face flushed and she looked sheepish. "Then, I went around to the back of the house to look for the tunnel entrance. The door was open, so I went in and followed it to the entrance of the hidden store-room."

"Charlotte! I cannot believe you would be so foolish!"

"I hoped to see something which would help clear Sir David's name!" She defended herself with some vehemence.

He was touched more than he could ever express to her—more of a reason for him to leave now. Perhaps he could spare her feelings from becoming more involved.

"When did Prescott find you, then?" Yardley continued his inquisition.

"Not until I was out on the beach and had already overheard his conversation with Dunn. He said I knew too much to live."

The Duke ran his hands through his hair. David did not think he had ever seen him so untidy.

"Fortunately, it is Prescott's body locked in the ice house—not yours. Wyndham and Harris have arrived and have gone to deal with the unpleasant duties arising from this mess. I thought it best to recuse myself, in the circumstances."

"Has someone been sent to arrest Howard? I suspect he can fill in the gaps, if he has not already heard the news and bolted," David suggested.

"Captain Harris has ordered the navy men to search for Dunn. Wyndham went to find the Revenue Officer to help him apprehend Howard."

"Unfortunately, Lord Wyndham will not be finding Officer Nibley." David moved forward.

Everyone looked at him in stunned silence, clearly trying to determine if he meant what they thought he did.

David continued. "In fact, his death is how I realized I had been sent to the Gap run to be out of the way. Dunn was there at an early stage—I suppose to confirm with me that all of the guests had departed from Langborn."

He cleared his throat. "It was low visibility—a perfect night for the trade—when I saw Dunn moving eastwards. Thinking it was odd, and being suspicious of the secret goods stashed here, I followed. I had been assigned as a look-out, so it was not obvious that I left."

He paused, trying not to visualize the scene in his mind. "I heard a commotion as Nibley fell—they had moved his trail markers and he had fallen off the cliff—but he was still hanging on when I saw Dunn step on his fingers and kick him over the edge."

Charlotte gasped.

"I had to make a choice," he continued, looking into the dancing flames of the fire. "I realized then what was happening. There was little hope for Nibley and I feared what might happen to Lady Charlotte." He looked away, afraid he had already revealed far too much.

Yardley nodded. "We need to send a messenger to the Home Office, and the King, immediately. This will need to be handled carefully, considering Prescott's position."

"I can take the message myself," David offered. "I can answer any questions first-hand and hopefully put this chapter of my life to rest."

He tried not to look, but he saw Lady Charlotte wince and turn away.

"I will be off at first light. I would like to bid my sister and niece farewell first, though."

"I will write the letters while you gather your belongings. It will be daylight soon."

David nodded as he turned to leave. Yes, this chapter was ending... but what next?

CHAPTER 16

I feel I am watching my life as a character in a play—as a mere puppet on a string. I can see what the ending will be, but I cannot stop the tragedy from occurring.—April 8

For Charlotte, the next few weeks flew by in a haze. At times, what had happened did not seem real, but for the pain in her heart. Wanting to put events behind her, she agreed to go to London for Letty's sake. However, by the time she was planning to leave, the Season ended. If she could not have Sir David, she would try travelling to see if her broken heart could be mended by a new adventure.

The new Season was to begin with the Cavenray ball and Charlotte assumed that Sir David would be there—or would he? Perhaps he thought his presence would taint Letty's come out. Before, Charlotte had always been able to put on a good face despite her spinster—and somewhat wallflower—presence in Society, but she did not know if she could present a façade any longer. Perhaps if Yardley realized her misery, he would let her go.

There had not been one single word of news from Sir David, other than he had received his pardon. She was truly happy for him, as he seemed to have changed from his younger days. Would he stay in England? Would he take a lower-born wife? Was it simply her lineage which held him back from her or was it something else? She could not imagine taking anyone else for a husband, feeling as she did about him. It would be wrong.

Needing to get away from the house for a while, Charlotte put on her dark green velvet pelisse and poke bonnet trimmed with a matching green ribbon. It had become a daily occurrence to escape the confines of the loving, happy family which threatened to smother her. It was repugnant to be jealous of her brother and his joy, and yet she had to get away so she did not become bitter about it.

It felt like freedom once she crossed the street into Hyde Park, escaping what seemed to be confining that freedom. How was she to manage for the entire Season? She had lost all pleasure in life—unable even to read a novel since that fateful day in February. Melancholy was such an overwhelming, ugly, consuming emotion. She realized she was in its grip, but she did not know how to remove its grasping fingers.

Bright yellow daffodils exploded in their magnificence along the pathways of the park. Nurses herded their charges along while older children played and giggled with their innocent and easy delight in games. None of it brought her joy any more.

Walking the gravel path beside the water, with no direction in mind, disdainful geese and scampering squirrels barely registered on the periphery of her notice. She was lost in thought when she saw him. He did not notice her and she was able to watch him at her leisure. It was a guilty pleasure, and she drank in the sight of him like a drug. He no longer looked like a pirate, but as the gentleman he was born to be. He had shaved and wore his fashionable attire with inherent grace and style. It might have been easier had he remained looking like a ruffian. Swallowing his rejection, when he looked a part of her world, was much harder.

Unable to pull away her gaze, she knew he must have felt her stare. His eyes met hers and she could sense his hesitation. There was no one else in the vicinity, but he merely inclined his head then kept going. She watched him until he was out of sight before she lowered her head and allowed herself to cry without restraint. She would have to wait before returning to the house because she dare not allow them to see her shame.

How could she continue this charade? Surely, her brother would listen to her pleas? He himself had hidden away in the country when he had been faced with scandal. Not that hers was a scandal, but her pain and embarrassment were genuine and she did not think she could pretend to the *ton* for day after tedious day. She could go to their mother in Malta. Benedict could not find any fault in that, could he?

When her tears had dried, she slowly ambled back to the house in time for a fitting at the modiste with Letty. She wanted her friend to succeed and she would do her best to make sure that happened.

No one seemed to notice Charlotte was abnormally quiet, as most of the attention was on Letty and her success. Afterwards, Charlotte could not even remember what colour her gown was and she could not bring herself to care.

Following the fitting, they were invited to take tea with the Duchess of Cavenray. Maili was sure to cheer her up.

Letty walked over to greet Maili, and whispered something in her ear. Charlotte pretended not to notice. Letty turned.

"I think I will take tea with mother since she did not feel like coming down today. I hope you do not mind?" she asked Charlotte.

"No, of course not. Please give her my regards and best wishes for a speedy recovery."

"Yes, of course. I will see you at dinner tomorrow?"

"I would not miss it," Charlotte answered with sincerity. It was difficult enough to be accepted into Society for those born to it. Letty would need all the support they could give her, being a Duke's natural child instead of his legitimate one.

When the door closed behind her friend, Maili came over to greet Charlotte. She took her hand and led her to a sofa. "Now please tell me what is happening. I have not seen you in weeks and I can see a great change in you. Letty said all of your gowns had to be taken up several inches."

Charlotte watched her hands. She could not quite meet Maili's direct gaze. Her friend had never been one to prevaricate—it was part of what she admired in her.

"It is true I have not been myself."

"Are you having nightmares? Is it because of what that horrid man tried to do to you?"

"I have had a few," she confessed, "but it is not the sole source of my melancholy." She was afraid to go near the water or dip her head under the water, but she did not wish to divulge the details of that awful night.

"Pray tell, Charlotte. You know I want to help you." Maili was searching her face for answers, and Charlotte feared her friend saw too much. However, if she could confide in anyone, it was the Duchess.

"It began at your wedding ball."

"My ball?" Maili's face showed utter consternation.

Charlotte gave a small, half-hearted laugh at her friend's bewilderment.

"I was on the terrace by myself, as I was wont to do. Having the freedom to do so after so many years of the chains of chaperonage, I escape whenever I can."

"Do go on." Maili indicated with her hand while her face seemed to reserve judgement.

"A man approached me and we spoke for a while. It was as though he understood me." She could hear the wistfulness in her tone.

"And?"

"And then he asked me to dance."

"How romantic!" Maili clasped her hands to her chest.

"It was the best few minutes of my life," Charlotte admitted.

Maili waited a few moments before begging, impatiently, "Well, who was this paragon of all romantic heroes?"

"He would not tell me. He said he was not a true gentleman and unworthy of my notice."

"If he was at my ball, I can assure you he was a suitable partner."

"Those were precisely my thoughts. However, when I began to question my brother and Jolie, as subtly as I could, I discovered it was Sir David Douglas."

"Deuce? Yes of course! I had not even considered..."

"You were a touch preoccupied, my dear."

Maili laughed. "I can see why he would be reticent at first, but now he has received his pardon, has retained the baronetcy, and is being lauded as a hero by the King. Whatever could be the reason now?"

"He still does not want me." Charlotte began to lose her composure, overthrown by that ugly combination of tears and trying to breathe.

Maili took her in her arms. "My dear, who could not want you? If I were a man, you would be my first choice!"

A giggle burbled out of Charlotte.

"There, there, that is better. We shall contrive something."

Charlotte leaned back and looked at her friend. She could see the wheels turning in her mind—those which seemed to become second nature to all wedded ladies the moment they said *I do*.

"No." She shook her head to emphasize her word.

Maili reached for a news-sheet. "Have you seen what the papers say?"

"I do not care." Charlotte had seen them...and had read every word twenty times.

"But he is a hero," Maili pleaded. "How could he not think he would be accepted now? Before all this, Cavenray, Dannon, Craig, and even your brother, vouched for him before the King!"

"I am happy for him, truly, but I do not care about those things. If he did not want me before, I cannot see that that will have changed."

"Oh, Charlotte. Please, we must try. I am certain it was his pride speaking. He would not think himself good enough for you, regardless of how matters now stand."

"No. I have been humiliated enough. I will not throw myself at him again. He said goodbye, and I could see by his actions today—I came across him in the park—that he meant it."

"If that is your wish, I will see you are not forced to be in his company at dinner. He must be there, as should you, for Letty's sake. I can ensure, however, you will not be escorted by, or seated beside, him."

"Thank you. It is all I could ask. I believe I will go and visit my mother in Malta for a while after the ball. Perhaps it will take the sharp edge from the pain."

"Oh, I hope so, dear Charlotte. If that is what you think best."

THIS WAS death by a thousand tiny paper cuts with vinegar poured on top. David would much prefer someone to impale him properly and get it over with. The anguish on Charlotte's face mirrored the agony in his heart. It was one of the hardest things he had ever done, to walk away from her in the park yesterday. How much easier it would have been to go to her and beg her to run away with him—but that was the most selfish act he could have ever committed. She deserved a far better life and reputation then he could give her; regardless of what the news-sheets were saying. He would be old news on the morrow, while the old scandals would continue to surface like a wart or the pox.

Tonight's ball would be pure torture yet again, for he knew she would be there. Once the ball was over, he would be free to leave. But he would never be free of her. He had already determined to go away for a time, in order to give her a chance to forget him and perhaps capture an appropriate suitor during the Season.

He really did not know where he would go, but he could not remain here and see her face every day. He suspected Davenport would soon ask for Letty's hand and he would not leave before that happy day.

The guests would soon be arriving for dinner; even so, he was downstairs early. He strolled through the house, still awed by the magnificence of it. This was how a Duke's daughter was raised and how she should continue to live.

The ballroom took his breath away. Even for an unsentimental reformed criminal, it was everything he had ever hoped Letty would have. Cavenray had spared no expense to make certain the *ton* knew she was his sister and fully accepted as such.

He stepped further into the room. Servants were placing finishing touches to the flower arrangements that perfumed the large space with the promise of spring and coloured the otherwise golden walls and wooden floor with bright sprays of pink, white and yellow. When the chandeliers were lit, it would be a spectacular display of spring and sunshine, which were everything Letty represented to him.

Cavenray had been so welcoming, would she have had a better life if he had taken her to him? Guilt assailed him but he had to push it aside. He had done the best he could and he knew better than to dwell on regrets. If he were to do so, he would have no further will to live. Continuing his life despite the pain was his penance, and he must do so while minimizing the pain to those he loved.

He heard the butler greeting someone and turned to see who had arrived: Yardley, from the sound of it. Was Charlotte there? He did not know if he could face her yet and remain strong. It would be far better for both of them if he could hide in the crowd.

Footsteps echoed in the hall behind him and he turned again to see Yardley surveying the room.

"Your Grace." He bowed.

"Sir David." The Duke held out his hand as he reached David's side. "I do think we are past formalities, no?"

David inclined his head with acknowledgement. He did not think the civilities would extend to wedding Lady Charlotte, unfortunately.

"Congratulations on your pardon. I have no doubt it is a relief."

"It is. I wish I could put it to rest in my mind."

"Hopefully, you will in due course. We found no other ties, beyond Dunn and Prescott, to a deeper organization. Reverend Howard's family had looked for a legitimate source to distribute the new cartridges, but no proper Briton would ever consent or admit to doing so publicly."

"I still cannot fathom what led Prescott to betray the country he swore to defend."

"Is not greed enough?" Yardley looked at him with eyebrows raised.

"It was certainly my downfall in my youth. Now that I have more than I need, it matters not."

"Would that we could all go back and undo the follies of our youth. I know I would."

It was David's turn to show surprise. A duke admitting to mistakes? This Duke had assuredly dispelled many of his misconceptions. "I have not properly thanked you for your assistance."

"And I have not properly thanked you for saving my sister's life."

"She would not have been in that position were it not for me."

Yardley let out a small chuckle. "An honourable sentiment, Douglas, but you and I both know my sister put herself in that position."

David gave a slight shrug of his shoulder. He was not going to argue. He still believed it was his fault she had been put at risk. He had never before felt true terror until that night, when he saw Prescott trying to force her under the water. *She could have died because of me.* His throat constricted at the thought.

"For what it is worth, I wanted to apologize. I was wrong about you, and if my sister wants you, I would be honoured to call you brother," the Duke said, a catch in his throat.

"I do not know what to say. I am beyond astonished by your words. Yet the fact remains I am the most unsuitable man for her."

"She does not seem to think so. I do not think so any longer. I will admit I misjudged you."

David shook his head. "Regardless of the honour she does me, I have to refuse. How could I bring my shame upon anyone I care for? Heap my sins upon the heads of my children?"

"It seems to me you have been burdened by your sins long enough. We are all ready to forgive you. When will you forgive yourself?"

"I do not know if I can," he whispered as he clinched his jaw to control his emotion.

They could hear the crowd gathering, and both turned to the door.

"One last favour, if you will. I am concerned about Charlotte. She has not been the same since the incident with Prescott, but she will not talk to me. Would you be willing to try?"

"I do not think that would be wise, under the circumstances. Perhaps she will confide in one of her friends?"

"Consider it. I have watched her riding herself silly in trying to forget. She no longer takes pleasure in food, conversation or novels. She stares out of the window for hours as though oblivious to the world around her. I want my sister back, and I think you are the man to do it."

"You have false hope in my abilities."

"I do not think I do." Yardley shook his hand with a smile and walked away, leaving David staring, dumbstruck, at a ship's itinerary left behind in his hand.

CHAPTER 17

Just once, I want the fairy tale to happen for me. I would give Romeo and Juliet a different ending, and make the world around them cease to matter. Instead, I am forced to try to salvage my dignity and do what is best for me.
—9 April

Through the entire dinner, David tried to muster his courage. He had been spared from sitting next to Charlotte, but he could see her. She was dressed in a lavender gossamer silk gown. She did look pale, and she was too thin. Her curls had been tamed into a simple chignon. Was heartache truly the cause or was it the after effects of almost dying? Whatever the reason, he felt the overwhelming urge to make it right.

She was still the most beautiful creature he had ever seen. Her new look would attract a great deal of attention. Even he knew she was very à la mode. During dinner, the other men had looked at her with appreciation and he felt another surge of jealousy. Could Yardley possibly be correct that she did want him, despite everything? Was it time to forget his past and make a new life with her?

What did Yardley mean by giving him this ship's passage? Did it mean Charlotte was to be on board and Yardley wanted him to go after her? Was she running away? So many questions...perhaps he could speak with her and convince her not to leave because of him. If anyone should leave, he should be the one to do so.

Too distracted to do justice to his dinner partner—a pretty young miss with dark ringlets and copious amounts of lace—who was flirting unabashedly and praising his heroism, he grew tempted to spill his wine in her lap. Placing another bite of glazed ham in his mouth, he nodded and smiled while mentally chewing over Yardley's approval. Is that what had been holding him back? Before, the Duke had not approved, therefore David was unworthy? He thought it was more than that, but he felt the smallest glint of hope for the first time.

Dinner was too long, yet too short. He was relieved to be rid of the tedious company, but he was not ready to make a decision. He was not so confident Charlotte would have him now. He had rejected her in a most complete manner. She had been willing to take him as he was before... but now, was he too late?

Fortunately, he was spared the receiving line. There were enough dukes, duchesses, lords and ladies for his presence to be superfluous. He found an alcove from which to observe, and decided to stay in the shadows unless it was necessary to perform some service for Letty. He had no wish to distract from her momentous day.

It felt as though there were thousands of people in the ballroom. Everyone had poured forth to see the old Duke's by-blow. It had been quite a story, last autumn, when her existence had been made known at the time of Lord Brennan's demise. Society thrived on a good scandal, and this family had provided endless pollen for it to buzz about for the entire Season.

David's gaze constantly drifted towards Charlotte. Like a fly to honey, he needed to know where she was at every moment. Was she happy? Was she being adored as she ought? He had not seen her dance yet. Had no one asked her? He could not imagine she would lack for partners with the attention she had stirred. He heard her name as often as he did Letty's and it was the latter's introduction to Society.

"Go and ask her, Sir David. You have not taken your eyes from her the entire evening," the Duchess of Yardley said, floating up beside him.

"What if she says no?" He did not pretend not to know of whom she was speaking.

"Make it so she cannot refuse," she answered simply.

"That is a low trick, even for me," he said appreciatively.

"Yardley is to dance with her next. It is not a dirty trick if done for the right reasons."

"Next will be my dance with Letty."

"So lead Letty to Yardley at the end of the set. Charlotte could hardly refuse you, and Yardley will dance with Letty. A perfect scenario, *non?*"

"Remind me never to cross swords with you, your Grace." She laughed and glided away, no doubt towards her next victim.

David led Letty out for a country dance. She looked radiant in a bright jonquil India muslin with a fine burgundy design woven through the fabric.

"I have hardly seen you in the last few weeks, Uncle."

"I hope that means you have been enjoying your time in London."

"It is quite different from our little island, is it not?"

"Yes. Do you miss it?" he asked, at once concerned.

"I miss the weather," she laughed. "But I would not trade my current situation for anything. I have you, but I also have my mother and brother."

"I am very sorry if I did wrong by you, Letty."

"Never apologize! I did not say that to make you suffer. I understand why you did what you did. I would not have lived to see this day otherwise."

He followed her gaze to where Mr. Davenport was dancing with the Duchess of Cavenray.

"Does he make you happy, Letty?"

"He does, and he welcomes Mother. I hope you are satisfied with the match."

"How could I not be? Your happiness is all I ever wanted for you."

"I know, Uncle. But what of you? You finally have what you have wanted for so long. Can you find your own happiness now?"

"I do not know if I am capable or deserving of your kind of happiness, my dear."

She cast him a look of reprimand.

"I do think some time away might be good for me. London is a difficult place to think."

"For one unused to such environs and such attention, yes," she agreed.

"I will return for the blessed event."

"Thank you, Uncle. That would mean the world to me, as would you finding your own happiness." She cast a meaningful look at Charlotte as he led her to where that lady was standing with Yardley.

He could see her straighten when he neared, as though bracing herself for battle. She looked so beautiful, he could scarce muster up the courage to ask her.

"Lady Charlotte, may I have this dance?" He held out his hand in invitation, and for a few brief moments, he thought she might actually refuse.

Charlotte quickly masked her surprise, though David could sense her trepidation. He had indeed placed her in a position where she could not refuse, not in front of so many watchful eyes. The strains of a waltz began and David had no doubt that had been arranged just as his partner had. There were greater forces at work here than his own desires.

Her hand was shaking when she placed it in his and he led her out to the floor. "Look at me, Charlotte."

Her eyes made it as far as his neckcloth. "I do not understand. Why are you doing this? There is no need to dance with me, for appearances or out of pity, even if Maili or Jolie tried to force you."

"I assure you this is nothing of the sort. I wish to dance with you." It was the truth. He placed his hand on her waist as the strings began to thrum the sounds of the waltz. It brought back the moment in

December, when he had first touched her... touched her while knowing what a mistake it was, besides being unworthy and unsuitable.

Due to some words of doubt placed into his head this evening, and watching her become a shadow of herself, he had gone against his better judgement and now held her in his arms. He was a weak man and did not know how many more times he could be strong enough to send her away.

Did she still want him? Would she tell him she was leaving?

"I suppose congratulations are in order, sir. You received your pardon and so maintain your title and the estate?"

She wished to make small talk. Very well. He could try.

"I did, thank you."

"Will you return to Crossings? That is the name of your estate, is it not?"

He nodded. "I have not yet decided. And yourself? Do you intend to enjoy the Season?" He still felt strongly that Lady Charlotte deserved better than he, and her deserving prince would arrive to sweep her away.

"I am leaving Town," she said, so quietly he had to strain to hear her words.

He looked down at her, but she still would not look him in the eye. He took his hand from her waist and lifted her chin.

"Not because of me, I hope? You should not be the one to leave."

"I intend to visit my mother. I have never met her new husband, nor seen the Continent. It seems as good a time as any." She left many words unsaid, he was sure.

"What of your suitors? I have seen many eligible gentlemen hovering near you tonight. May I say also, you look beautiful, although I fear you are fading away before my eyes. I thought you perfect the way you were. Are."

She shook her head as if fighting off tears. He took the opportunity to twirl her out to the terrace where it had all begun for them.

"Please take me back inside." Her chin quivered as tears streamed down her face. Is this what he did to her?

"What can I do? What can I say to make you happy again?" He felt desperate to make her smile, to laugh. If he could take that night in December back, he would do so and stay out of her life.

"Please do not do this."

"I never meant to hurt you, Charlotte."

"It is too late for that."

CHARLOTTE BRUSHED past David and went straight for the front door. She would send a note of apology later, but she could not stay here one moment longer. She would send the carriage back for Benedict and Jolie.

Thank God she already had a passage to Malta. She did not think she could have made herself leave him otherwise. Why was he being nice to her tonight? And why must love hurt so much? If he had truly reciprocated her feelings, he would have fought for her instead of trying to encourage her towards other men. Could he not understand there were no other men; that there never would be?

Knowing that, day by day, the pain would become a little more bearable was small comfort at the moment. When she arrived back at the town house, Chapman had already packed her trunks. The maid helped Charlotte out of her gown and she slid into her bed without a word to the woman. Chapman had been with her long enough to know better than to shatter her thinly veiled composure by talking.

The next morning she dressed in a violet travelling costume and tried to greet the day with new optimism. She would have to say farewell to some friends and family, for there were a few to whom she could not simply send a note. No one would understand why she had to leave. Even her brother had objected but would not hold her back. She had seen the pity in his eyes and that was the hardest to bear. Thankfully, he had not renewed his offer of parading more suitors in front of her in the way he had attempted his own marriage selection.

Charlotte had to admit she had enjoyed the surprise on her friends' faces when she announced she was leaving. She never did anything unexpected and certainly never on impulse. Until the moment she stepped out of the carriage onto the docks, she really had not considered what she was doing. Chapman had groaned and objected since informed where they were going, but the maid had refused to stay behind when Charlotte had offered.

When tears threatened, Charlotte forced herself to think about blue waters, sunshine and warm breezes. Her mother had written also of delicious foods and fine wines. Perhaps that would cause Charlotte's appetite to return. She now possessed the body she had always dreamed about, yet it was no comfort for her aching soul.

Had *The Jolie* not gone down in flames, thanks to her, she would have been sailing on her brother's yacht. Instead, he had arranged passage on *The Wind*, owned by Lord Harris, Jolie's sister's husband. He was to captain the ship himself.

Looking up at the large three-masted ship, she surveyed her home for the next few weeks before boarding. Seamen were swarming the deck and ropes, preparing to set sail, and her trunks were being carried across the gangway. With one last farewell to Benedict, she crossed the plank herself, hoping it was a bridge to a new beginning.

Her wood-panelled cabin was fine enough, with a small bunk and dressing table, and she did not care who the other passengers were as she had no intention of mingling. Three weeks of moping in her cabin should see her sufficiently sick of it in time to greet her mother properly with a smile.

As the boat began to sail, she was unprepared for the sensation of swaying and bobbing as they left the harbour. She found she could not walk without falling into something, so she sat on her bunk to catch her balance. At the moment, she could not bear to watch what she was leaving behind. She knew he would not be there waiting for her.

Lady Harris had gifted Charlotte a journal, in which to keep track of her travels. Anjou mentioned having been given one at a similar time in her life and it had helped her through similar trials. Perhaps it would help. Charlotte had always dabbled in her diary, but had never done any serious writing or pouring out of her heart. She always suspected someone would read her innermost thoughts some day, if she did—and that was an unnerving thought.

"Who cares if they do?" she asked aloud. If journaling was the way to mend her spirit and find herself again, she would happily dribble whatever came to mind onto the pages of this book.

Unfortunately, she stared at the page, unable to think of anything to write beyond the obvious, and the words felt too mundane to bother. She was escaping her life on a ship to Malta. She had no more dreams at the moment except to pray she could hope again some day.

The pen dropped from her hand, splattering ink across the blank page... one large blob that spread and faded into several tiny droplets. Perhaps it was a metaphor for her life.

Thinking again about her loss only made her angry. She would have given up her title and wealth for a chance at happiness. The only reason Charlotte could see which made any sense, was that he did not consider her worth the sacrifice. The bitter realization nearly doubled her over with agony. It was finally real—no longer a fantasy.

Staring blankly at herself in the small glass, she did not recognize the woman looking back at her. She was a stranger who appeared to represent everything Charlotte was growing to hate. She could not look any longer. Turning the mirror face down in disgust, she huddled into the small seat in the hull and stared at nothing. For several days, she existed thus. It was as though her mind could not bear the pain and ceased to function. She no longer cared what became of her. Although Chapman would come in and fuss over her and force a few bites of food down, Charlotte barely tasted anything.

The cabin door opened and Chapman set a tray down with a loud thud. "I've had enough of this mopin', your ladyship. You have missed the entire coast of France and we are alongside Portugal already. Now, I've had Cook prepare your favourite pudding, which you will eat, and then I am takin' you up to the deck for some fresh air. Now, will you feed yourself or shall I do it?" She put her hands on her hips and scowled down at Charlotte as though she were still in the nursery.

Charlotte merely glared in response, wondering if it was worth the effort to fight or just comply. Chapman took a spoonful of blanc-mange and handed it to her. Charlotte took the spoon and thrust it in her mouth like a petulant child. It was delicious, she had to admit, as she reached for another bite-sized amount. It tasted just like Cook's from Langborn. The maid looked on with an expression of triumph. While Charlotte ate, Chapman pulled out a day gown of pale blue muslin suited to a London drawing room in summer. There was no one to impress, but she still had no will to argue over trivial things. Perhaps the sunshine would feel nice.

Standing to allow the maid to complete her ministrations, Charlotte noticed some little, intricate woodcarvings lining her dressing table.

"What are those?" she asked.

"One has been delivered each day since we left, my lady."

"From whom? For me?"

"I cannot say as I know, my lady." She finished with Charlotte's laces and directed her to sit down.

"Does someone on board carve these?"

"There is certainly extra time on our hands, even for the crew. I saw some of the men knitting and mending."

Charlotte picked up one of the carvings and fingered it tenderly. They were some kind of creatures of the sea, she supposed. She had read of some of them but had not seen them.

A dolphin. An otter. A seal. A turtle. The one she held was some type of bird she could not name.

"These are exquisite. See if you can discover who carved them."

"Yes, my lady," Chapman replied as she forced Charlotte's hair into a plain chignon.

The warm breeze that hit Charlotte's face, as she climbed the ladder to the deck, felt invigorating. Then the sunshine felt like an assault on her eyes after so many days in a dark cabin. It was glorious. Once her eyes adjusted, the first things she noticed were rugged cliffs along a coastline and turquoise waters. She had never seen water so vivid and colourful. She now understood what had lured her mother away. She did not think she would ever tire of looking at it. Is this what she had missed by sulking in her cabin? Were those creatures someone had lovingly carved for her what she could have been seeing if she had been watching? A small glimmer of renewal began to take shape within her breast. And then she turned around. Were her eyes deceiving her?

CHAPTER 18

My own fairy tale, written by myself, would now include a handsome pirate, of course, to save me from my treachery and sail me away to a tropical island to know neither cold nor heartache ever again. Now I question whether "tis better to be left than never to have been loved". Perhaps in a decade I may look back at this with good humour, once the pain is not so new.—15 April

How much longer would she stay in her cabin? Each subsequent day, David was tempted to barge in and throw himself at her feet. It had made sense to come after her at the time, but now he was questioning his hasty decision. Pacing back and forth across the deck, he wondered whether or not to disembark at the next port and find another ship to save inflicting his presence upon her.

The truth was, his objections from the beginning were still valid. He still had a criminal past, and he knew she could find a better husband. He had allowed Yardley's approval and the King's pardon to cloud his decisions. Now, here he was, on a ship bound for Malta, chasing after a woman whose heart he had broken. He could not blame her if she did not want to see him again or give him a second chance, but he had to try. The alternative was too painful to consider.

The vast ocean and its depths could not solve his dilemma, and he had asked the deep blue many times over the past days. Leaning over the railing, he put his head in his hands. He felt near to desperation. Charlotte was worth fighting for, but was it beyond hope?

"Sir David?"

"Lady Charlotte?" He turned and looked at the vision before his eyes. It was such sweet sorrow. His first impulse was to throw his arms around her and ease the pain she was so clearly feeling—the pain he had caused by what he had done to her. She did not look well. Her hair was pulled back into a severe knot and she was ghostly pale with dark circles under her eyes.

"What are you doing here?" she asked, as though trying to determine if he was real or an illusion.

"Your brother booked me a cabin."

Surprise registered on her face. "Why? I do not understand. Why did you come?"

"Because I knew you would be here."

She shook her head, looking confused. He could not blame her for not comprehending. He watched her maid slip away.

"You have been on board the whole time?"

"Yes."

Charlotte walked over to the railing a few feet away from him and looked out into the water. "I came to forget."

"Forget what?" he asked softly.

"You, if I am being honest. I am such a fool." She swallowed hard. "Never before had a man looked at me the way you did or made me feel so alive. I naïvely assumed that it meant you felt the way I did. I practically threw myself at your feet. I finally realized you did not return my regard, so I left to lick my wounds in private. Must I ask again, why have you come?"

"Charlotte, it was never meant to be like that." He reached for her and she flinched.

"I cannot see what has changed. You had been pardoned when last I saw you, yet it seemed not to be enough, then."

"While it is true I am still unworthy of you, and no doubt should

159

have stayed away, I found I could not. At the ball, I had several revelations."

She turned sideways and finally looked up to meet his gaze.

"The first was, no matter what Society considers me now, you did not care when I was nobody; when I had nothing to recommend me—rather the opposite. Secondly, I found I was accepted and had been pardoned by the King—but *you* had accepted me before. Thirdly, your brother approves of me as a match for you and that matters to me more than it should."

"Why?" she whispered, searching his face.

"This entire time, I have used his disapproval as validation of my unworthiness..." He stepped closer to her. "...but after he gave me passage on your ship, I could not stay away. Can you forgive me, Charlotte? Am I too late?"

She inhaled deeply. "How can I know you will not change your mind? I do not think I can bear to suffer this again. Over and over, I gave you my heart and you kept handing it back to me."

"I did not do so because it was what I desired. I did not want to put you in danger. You refused to see what a poor bargain I am and I thought to convince you. What would you have done in my position?" He held out his hands, begging the question.

Her lips thinned and she shook away tears that were streaming down her cheeks. "I am not sure, but I believe I would have accepted the gift and cherished it for the rest of my life."

He smiled at her doubtfully and stepped forward with his hand out.

She hesitated, as he expected she would.

"May I court you properly?"

"Why bother?" she asked dryly. "You know my heart is yours for the asking. I happen to know the Captain. We could marry now."

"You little minx. I would like some time to show you what you mean to me. And I do not think I would like to answer to his Grace if we eloped. You may still change your mind."

"Please do not tell me you mean to consult him on every detail of our marriage. I believe he already consented by sending you on this ship."

"I suppose he did," he said, contemplating the deliciousness of such a notion. "No, I will not let you deter me from doing things properly. Will you dine with me tonight?"

"You are determined on this?"

"I am more in earnest than I have ever been in my life."

He took her hand and kissed the tips of her fingers before tucking them into his arm. She leaned her head on his shoulder and they stood together in peaceful harmony, watching the waves ripple behind the ship, for some time. David felt a serenity he had never known—a rightness with the world and God that he knew he did not deserve. It was selfish of him to have come after Charlotte, but he would spend the rest of his life making it up to her.

HE HAD COME FOR HER. He had come for her! He said he wanted to court her and he had Yardley's blessing. Charlotte could not believe this was real. It must be some strange dream in which she felt awake and everything seemed real—yet it was not. Why had Chapman not told her Sir David was on board? No matter; he was here now. She danced and twirled excitedly about the tiny cabin. How could her emotions go from one extreme to another in a matter of minutes? She had been in the depths of despair less than an hour ago and now she was about to burst from happiness. Admittedly, she tended to be a pessimist, given to looking suspiciously for an ulterior motive. She supposed things could still go wrong, but since they had come this far, and over the biggest hurdle, she felt cautiously optimistic. Although, it then occurred to her, he had not mentioned love or marriage—she had. Frowning, she stopped and considered. *No, no, no,* the little voice in her head said. Now was not the time to think but simply enjoy.

Calling for Chapman and requesting a bath—if there were such luxuries on ships—she wanted to look her best. It seemed an age until he came to escort her to dinner. She had not yet been to the dining room and did not know if there were other guests on board or not. Sir David led her up a ladder of sorts, to the deck where they had met before. It was a warm, balmy evening and the sky was a pinkish purple hue as the sun hung low over the horizon.

A small table with two chairs was sitting on the deck near the fo'c'sle. It was covered with a white cloth and candles had been lit. A deck-hand held a chair for her and she sat down.

"Is this the dining room?" she asked, giving her escort a pleased smile.

"It is the one I prefer. I thought you might enjoy the fresh air after being in your cabin for several days."

"It is perfect."

"The food on board is excellent. I did not have such exquisite fare on my Atlantic crossings. Your brother sent along one of his cooks."

The waiter began to serve them several courses as though they were in a normal home.

"This is a feast!" Charlotte exclaimed as dish after succulent dish was placed before her. "How did you know all my favourites? White soup and cheesecake!"

"Your maid was a wonderful resource."

"Why did she not tell me you were on board?"

"I asked her not to. I knew you needed time."

Charlotte inclined her head. It was true; she might not have been as receptive at first. Then it dawned on her. "Are you the one who carved the animals?"

He replied with a simple smile. "My father taught me. It gave me time to think while I waited for you. I want us to take the time to know each other better. I want you to know what a bad bargain I am while you still have a chance to change your mind," he continued.

"You think you can scare me away now?"

"I still think you might come to your senses. I think you will wake up one day and someone will hurt you by gossiping about me; or even with the things they will doubtless say about our children."

"I do not deny that our world is full of malicious fools, and I do not deny that your past is likely to be spoken of again. However, it will only be of significance if we allow it to be. There will be few who will speak against us when we have the support of so many of Society's foremost families."

"That much is true. I admit it is astonishing to feel their presence behind me."

"Moreover, I do not need Society to be happy, David. I would prefer not to choose between you and my family, but if there came a time when we felt it necessary to move away, I would go with you."

"I still do not understand why you care for me so, but I will not question it."

"Alas, that is an answer I can easily provide." She smiled.

His eyes moved swiftly to meet hers.

"You saw *me* when no one else did. You brought me to life when I did not know I had yet to live." She shook away the tears forming as she struggled for composure.

"You have not allowed others truly to see you before. You hide your light."

She took a deep breath and he clasped her hands in his across the table.

"I can only be grateful the other men were blind or you would not be here. You also had faith in me when others did not... and now, what I had not dared to dream might be possible."

Music began to play softly around them and Charlotte started. She had not noticed anyone joining them on the deck. A few of the deck-hands had instruments which resembled violins and they were playing a melody that faintly resembled a waltz.

"You have thought of everything," she said softly. Feeling bashful, she lowered her lashes as she smiled.

"Lord Harris has a very diverse crew," he replied with a wink. Rising, he held out his hand. "Lady Charlotte, may I have this dance?"

The available deck was small and the waters were calm, though his strong arms steadied her when she stumbled. She inhaled deeply of the warm air and his spicy scent that made her world feel all was as it should be. It was as magical as their first dance on the terrace when he was but a stranger, several moons ago. It was funny how, since he had come into her life, she now sensed time according to the moons. There was a mysterious draw to the moon and she could see why history and poets lauded its powers.

She was enchanted and never wanted this euphoric feeling to end. When the music ceased after a few songs, they stopped swaying and the musicians discreetly left them. David held her in his arms and looked into her eyes, into her being.

Cradling her face with gentleness, he gazed at her with what she could only describe as affection, perhaps even more. She was barely coming to understand her own feelings.

His lips descended upon hers with tender reverence. A warm fluttering sensation spread through her body and she felt alive again in the way she had experienced with none but him. Her lips tingled as she explored the taste and feel of him. She opened her eyes, so she might watch and memorize his dark lashes against his skin and the way his brow furrowed when he concentrated.

Was she opening herself up only to be rejected again? Or would he finally be hers to have and to hold? She did not want to think, simply feel... and this felt right. When his lips moved away, she let out a small whimper of protest. He chuckled as he continued to shower her face, ears and neck with soft caresses. His forehead touched hers and their eyes met.

"We keep finding ourselves under the moon and stars."

"My favourite place."

David chuckled. "They say honest work is not done at night. At least, that is what I heard often of the free trade, though you can see more than you think in the dark."

"And you cannot see the stars without the darkness."

"It is where I found my north star."

When he finally led her back to her cabin, she did not want to continue courting for her mind was quite made up, but she knew it was for the best. He opened her door for her and reached inside to turn up the flame in her lamp. She stood on her tiptoes in order to give him one last kiss good night, but before her lips met his, he shouted, "What the devil?"

CHAPTER 19

I have ceased to be amused. I now have my handsome pirate and forces still work to keep us apart.—16 April

Chaos ensued when people heard David shout. Every available deckhand came running to see what was wrong. Charlotte tried to control her shaking limbs. It would be much more pleasant to think a strong wave had overturned everything in her cabin, but the seas had been calm and the act had been committed on purpose.

"What has happened?" Lord Harris's deep voice boomed when he arrived. He took in the situation in seconds. Turning to his crew, he demanded them to search for a stowaway.

"You think someone sneaked on board?" David asked.

"I would put my name on the line for any of my crew. You and Charlotte are the only passengers."

"Then this was deliberate." The reality of the ramifications began to set in. "Thank God I was not in here at the time!" she exclaimed.

"Hopefully the criminal was searching for something, not intending to harm you," Harris said.

"But I do not understand. What could I have that someone would sneak on board to steal?"

"Jewels?" Harris suggested.

"We will need to see if anything was stolen," David said.

"I did not bring anything of significant worth." She dismissed the idea.

"Maybe the thief did not know that and took his chances. Let us put the cabin to rights and see if anything is missing."

Her maid, Chapman, had already begun. The furniture was nailed to the floor, and Charlotte had not brought too much luggage, so it was not long before everything had been returned to normal—except for her insides. She felt violated. Someone—some stranger—had looked through all her personal belongings.

David placed an arm around her and held her tight as if guessing her thoughts. His hand stroked soothingly up and down her back and she did not want him ever to let go.

"Why would someone do this? It makes no sense," she asked.

"Sometimes you never discover a reason. Most criminal acts stem from either greed or desperation."

"I cannot think greed alone could be the explanation for someone risking such a dangerous deed. Are any of the other cabins ransacked?"

Lord Harris answered, "No."

"Nothing seems to be missing, my lady," Chapman said. "Even your jewels are still here." She held up a pouch of trinkets which were worth a small fortune, even though they were not ducal heirlooms.

"'Twas not greed, then." Charlotte remarked. "Could this be some kind of a warning? Is there more to the smuggling than we thought?" she asked with genuine consternation.

"Why not me, in that case?" David asked. "Surely their grudge would be with me, not you?"

"It was because of me that Prescott died. If I had not struggled with him, he would have got away," she explained.

"No, you cannot think that. We had other measures in place to catch them."

"Did they know that? If Colonel Prescott was only one of the villains involved in the scheme, there could be others."

David shook his head. "We have not found anything beyond Colonel Prescott. He had the connections in the Home Office. He was clearly the mastermind. And you saw what happened to the boat Dunn was on."

"Was he ever found, though?"

A pregnant pause ensued before he answered, with obvious reluctance.

"Not to my knowledge," David said, looking at Lord Harris, who also gave a small shake of his head.

"It is not likely that he ever will be found, Charlotte. The sea would have carried his body far away very quickly. Only a few pieces of the ship even made it back to shore," Harris explained.

Charlotte was only mildly reassured. It seemed too much of a coincidence to discount the fact that Dunn had somehow escaped or been rescued. The men probably suspected the same, but were trying to protect her *delicate sensibilities*—again.

"There has to be a reason for this to have happened."

"We will be done with searching the ship soon," Harris replied.

"Would you prefer to exchange cabins with me?" David offered. "Mine is not quite so handsome, but if you will feel safer you are welcome to it."

"No, thank you. Chapman will sleep in here with me. If you had ever seen her deal with a mouse, you would fear for anyone who dare cross her."

Chapman let out a muttered, "Humph."

The men laughed at the comic relief. Charlotte had always found humour useful as a protective mechanism to hide her true feelings. Hopefully, they would not see through this flimsy barrier to her true thoughts. Nonetheless, there had to be more to this than they knew, which meant they were still not safe. The question she could not answer was what could the smugglers want from her? Or did they seek to terrorize her by scaring her to death; to keep her from sleeping as well as causing her to jump at every shadow? It was an effective means of punishment, she had to admit. Would Dunn take such risks, however?

His livelihood would have been stripped from him, and he would be desperate, which meant he needed something. This was not mere punishment. He either thought she had something or thought to gain from her.

It was not a settling realization as she tried to find sleep. Chapman was already well past forty winks by the sounds of her snores and Charlotte sighed with frustration. This was why she avoided sharing her room with her old nurse. As much as she wanted to go and find David or Harris to see what had been discovered, she was more afraid of walking about the ship, alone, at night.

DAVID JOINED HARRIS in his cabin after he had seen Charlotte safe inside hers, with Chapman ready to defend her mistress to the hilt.

"This is a development I had not anticipated," David said, sinking into a chair.

"Nor any of us," Harris agreed as he poured two glasses of brandy and handed one to David before sitting in the other armchair.

"It must be Dunn."

"But how did he know she would be on a ship and which one?"

"We hardly kept it a secret. We did not know we needed to. Certainly everyone at the house in London would have known, and likely Langborn as well."

"Do you think he has been on board since England?" David considered.

"Unlikely. We stopped once, along the Coast of France, to pick up some cargo. He could have easily disguised himself and come on board. My crew did not know to be suspicious."

"If he were set on vengeance, why wait until now? Why not act sooner?"

"Perhaps it was a target of opportunity—a coincidence even. We have no proof that Dunn was our man."

"Do you think he is still on the ship?"

"Only if he is waiting for a noose around his neck. However, at this point he has little to lose." Harris swirled his drink.

"Indeed. I think he is looking for something specific." Harris's eyebrows elevated in question. "He did not take any valuables, and he waited until Charlotte left her cabin—which she had not done for nearly the first week of the journey. Either he waited in hiding, on the ship somewhere, or he joined us at the last port."

"Therefore, you conclude Charlotte has something he wants. But did he find it or not? Will we be safe, or will we be stalked by this unscrupulous murderer until he gets what he wants?"

"Charlotte has no idea, I would bet on it. I think we had best hope your men find him on board, or we may never know and she will never feel safe again. I felt that way about Brennan, even when I was in the Indies. I had no doubt he knew where I was and I was always looking over my shoulder."

"I fear you are right. It is an unfortunate situation. I cannot think his chances of jumping ship would be very successful, but he would have needed a plan. You cannot simply ransack a cabin on a ship in the middle of the ocean and not expect someone to be looking for you afterwards," Harris noted dryly.

"Do you think he had a rowing boat, or could he have used one of yours to escape?" David suggested.

"He could not have taken one of mine, they are stored on deck," Harris said quickly, but he was pondering the matter. There was a small crease between his brows. "I suppose there is a slight chance; if he had an accomplice, he could have managed it. We are in calm seas and not too far from land."

There was a sharp knock on the door. "Enter," Harris called.

Connors, the first mate, entered. He was the one David had seen taking the helm when Harris was not. He was young and weathered like most sailors, but looked capable. "There is no sign of him, Captain."

"Any sign of him having stowed away anywhere?"

"None. I did not think that likely from the beginning, but I cannot see how someone could have boarded without our knowledge while at sea."

"We were just contemplating that very thing."

"There was only a small amount of time, while Charlotte was out of the cabin. How would he have known if he had not been on board, watching her movements?" David asked.

"It seems much too unlikely to be coincidence, since she had not left her cabin before."

"Thank you, Connors. Can you keep one man watching over the cabins in case our man has eluded us?"

"Aye aye, sir."

After the first mate left, Harris looked at David. "I think Charlotte is going to have to determine what Dunn is looking for. There has to be something he wants from her."

"Or, he at least thinks she has. She had no dealings with Dunn to my knowledge and only a few moments with Prescott—until the moment they were struggling in the water."

"Could Charlotte have, unknowingly, taken something from Prescott during their struggle? Or unwittingly dislodged something and Dunn is convinced she has it?" Harris continued to think aloud.

"The devil! That must be it. We have to catch him!" David pounded his fist on his leg.

"What if he has already found it?" Harris refilled his drink.

"I cannot believe it would be so easy."

"Do you want me to turn the ship around and go back to the nearest port—try to search for him?" We can go into deeper waters until Gibraltar. It would make it less likely he could give chase. Afterwards, we will be negotiating around shoals and reefs as we approach Malta."

"No. I do not want to risk Charlotte. If he does not have what he wants, he will not stop."

"Still assuming this is Dunn we are talking about, we need to think like him. What would cause him to come after her? There is perhaps only one answer."

"Money." David nodded.

"A key of some sort? A treasure map?" Harris chuckled.

"The likelihood that anything would have survived on her person, in the water, is minuscule. He is desperate enough to take that chance, I gather."

"You used to run in his world. What could he be after? Where would payments get made for receipt of goods?"

"We did not get paid until the job was done. The ammunition was discharged on the ship, so the goods were not delivered."

"So, the operation failed. Was that everything?"

"Actually, no. There were guns. They buried them on the beach that night. If he went back in and uncovered them and carried on with the exchange, he would be looking for the payment, if he did not receive it at the time. We disrupted their plans and they had to move quickly, possibly disrupting their usual method."

"I still do not understand why he thinks Charlotte would have something. It makes no sense. I assume we will know in time. The truth will always out unless he has already found what he needs."

David sighed. "So much for a relaxing wooing of my future bride."

Harris laughed. "What is the fun in that? Did your candlelight dinner go well?"

"I believe so. She said we could marry now because she knew the Captain."

"This Captain values his life more than marrying Yardley's sister in a private wedding. I have a feeling that the family will all be joining us, soon."

"I do not know whether I should laugh or cry at that news." David frowned.

"Having married into the family some years ago, might I suggest you take the path of least resistance. As with sailing, going against the wind is futile."

"The wind always wins?"

"Exactly." He leaned over and clinked his glass with David's. "To your future with Charlotte. I promise it will be worth it."

CHAPTER 20

Is there anything more wracking to the nerves than for someone to think you know something and you do not? Before, I have only experienced this frustration with dim-witted suitors or spiteful gossips. Now I am being chased by a hardened criminal for it, and it is most unsettling. I would gladly part with what he wants if only I knew what it was.—17 April

The next day, the sun still rose and life seemingly returned to usual. There was little to do but wait. Even though things looked normal, Charlotte could see that there was a new sense of watchfulness about the ship.

"Good morning," she said to Sir David and Lord Harris. They were on the quarter-deck, conversing, but stopped and gave her bows of greeting when she approached.

"I gather our perpetrator was not found?" she asked.

"Unfortunately not," David replied.

"And have you decided to do anything about it? Do you have any idea who it could be?" She watched their faces closely for any sign that they might be hiding something from her. Men tended to do that—at least her brother did—and she was suspicious.

"We think it very likely that Captain Dunn did not die in the fire as we suspected," David said frankly.

Charlotte was astonished. "I do not understand. Do you think he followed us from England?"

Lord Harris blew out a breath. "Honestly, we are not certain. We found no signs of anyone stowing away, but the idea that he followed us in a ship, unbeknownst to us, and escaped the same way, is unfathomable. My crew has too much experience to allow anyone to sneak up on them. We would not have survived the years of war and privateering for so long, otherwise."

She nodded as she tried to assimilate what they were telling her. They remained silent, still watching her.

"Irrespective of the manner, someone slipped on board and ransacked my cabin. What do you think he was looking for?"

"Charlotte, can you recall your time with Prescott? I know it is painful to think about, but was there anything at all that he might have said to you or that you could have taken from his person during your struggle?"

"You think I have something he wants. This was not just a way to punish me for ruining his livelihood?"

"It could well be that, and we will not know for certain unless he comes back again. He may have found what he wanted last night."

Charlotte sat down and closed her eyes, trying to cast her mind back to that dreadful night.

"The house was empty, and I heard a noise behind the secret door in the library," she said, eyes closed, picturing that night. "I went looking for the outside entrance and found the door open. I went through the tunnel until I found the store-room, but it was empty. Two men passed me, but did not see me, so I followed them when I thought it was safe. I continued on through the tunnel until I reached the ravine, and then kept walking out onto the beach. I found a small crevice to hide in, and noticed the men burying bags in the sand. I assumed it was the guns you had found in the hidden store-room." She took a deep breath as she remembered, but kept her eyes closed. "I felt the water come over my boots as the tide began to come in. I did not see you, Sir David, as I had gone to try to find something to help you. I began to turn around when I overheard them speaking about the new type of gun cartridge and realized it was all hidden on my brother's yacht. I knew that was the missing information and I grew anxious to return to the house to find Benedict."

She inhaled a ragged breath. "That is when an arm grabbed me from behind. I immediately began to panic. I recalled Sir David's warnings that these men would not hesitate to kill me. I did not know who it was at first, of course. We struggled. The other men began to leave in small rowing boats and I called out for their help—but it was as if no one heard me. Prescott made some type of call similar to the ones the men use when hunting. There was an answering call and I saw *The Jolie* come into view. I had not noticed it before, due to the dense fog. That was when I knew he was going to kill me. He began to drag me through the water towards the ship. He tried to force me under the water and I kicked him as hard as I could. He released his grasp long enough for me to get my head above the water again. I had a small pistol Benedict had bought for me and I knew I needed to retrieve it before all was lost. I cannot remember how I managed to snatch it from inside my cloak. I did not know if it would be dry or not, but it was my only chance."

She paused to compose herself and felt David's arm come around her in gentle reassurance.

"Take your time. I know it is painful to remember."

"But there must be something—some little detail—I am forgetting."

"Perhaps. It is likely there was some small thing he said that is the key—or even, mayhap, something you tore from him during the struggle.

She wrinkled her face with the effort as she thought about those terrifying moments. "I do remember his neckcloth ripping..." She shook her head. "I do not recall dislodging anything from him, though."

"Could something have landed in your cloak?"

She opened her eyes and gave him a look which she hoped conveyed the foolishness of his question.

"You are welcome to look, but the odds are more favourable to beat the house at a gaming hell."

They all laughed at the analogy. "True, but it would be stupid not to even look."

"Then send for Chapman. She might have burned it at Langborn. She was complaining about my gown being ruined."

Harris turned and instructed one of his seamen to fetch her maid and the cloak.

"So after you went for your gun, what happened next?"

"It was over with very quickly. Sir David shot Prescott and I shot at the yacht."

"Why did you shoot the yacht?" Harris asked.

"Because I did not want them to get away. I did not even know if my gun was too wet to fire, but I had nothing to lose. I knew I had one chance and the heat from the powder could cause a spark, which I discovered after setting a target on fire when practising with Benedict. If a spark could ignite a target, then it was probable that it would ignite paper cartridges and gunpowder on the ship. It was more effective than I had imagined in the few seconds I had to do so. Had I had the luxury, I would have aimed at Dunn. It was too dark to make out anything other than the hull through the fog."

"You kept a ship-load of cartridges out of the hands of our enemies, Charlotte. We will sort this out and capture whoever is still after that unknown something."

Chapman climbed onto the deck, holding Charlotte's cloak across her arms.

"I was not sure if you had burned it," Charlotte said to the maid.

"I did burn the dress," the maid replied with a laboured sigh. "If it had been any of your other cloaks, it would not have survived."

"Would you like to do the honours?" She held the cloak, which was made of oilcloth, out to Sir David.

He shook his head. "You are more familiar with the pockets in your own garments, my lady."

"Very well." She began searching through each opening in the cloak, but all were empty. "This is where I hid the gun," she demonstrated the hidden compartment within the breast, "which explains how it stayed dry in the water."

"What are you looking for, my lady?" Chapman asked.

"We do not know. Did you remove anything from the pockets of the cloak or gown while at Langborn?" Charlotte asked the maid.

"No, my lady. Nothing at all."

"It would have been too easy," Charlotte mused, trying to hide her disappointment. "We think the butcher, Mr. Dunn, was the one behind rummaging through my cabin. He was the leader of the smuggling gang, as you no doubt already know."

"I think everyone knew that, my lady. Cook was right put about when she heard he had died. You think he is still alive?"

"It is possible, though we have not seen him. Why was Cook upset?"

"Why, he is her brother. You did not know?"

Charlotte shook her head in disbelief. "It is a wonder I was not poisoned."

Harris hastened off down the companionway without a word.

"Dunn probably bullied her when the house was empty or helped himself through the secret passage." David paced the small area of deck in front of her.

"Why would he wait until now?" Charlotte questioned.

"Desperation. We foiled his money-making scheme." David answered.

"If only I knew what he hoped to find, I would gladly part with it to be rid of the fear of not knowing what comes next."

"Thank you, Chapman. That will be all."

Harris returned, pulling a reluctant cook up the companionway. As he halted before them, he continued to hold the woman's arm.

Charlotte gasped. "I cannot believe it! Would you care to explain your part in all of this?"

Cook shook her head and began to sob. "I had no idea what 'e was planning. Honest! 'E said 'e wished to make a new life somewhere, so I let him stow in me little berth. But 'e is gone now. 'E jumped ship last night."

"And before, at Langborn?"

A guilty look passed over the cook's face.

"Sending me for a ham was a code, was it not?" David asked.

She nodded. "But 'e wasn't gonna hurt nobody. I just let 'im know iffin guests arrived."

"Take her away," David said to Harris. "We will have to deal with her when we land."

"I'm right sorry, my lady. I didn't know 'e was gonna 'urt ye."

Charlotte could not look at the snivelling woman, she was so disgusted.

"Do not fret, my dear. We will come about. There may not be anything to find, anyway. Dunn might be imagining the whole."

Charlotte nodded, but could not help but feel she held the missing link.

DAVID SAT CARVING ANOTHER CREATURE—A fish—not one of his more original creations, but it helped pass the time. He often did his best thinking when he was working with his hands, allowing his mind time to settle and reflect on the problem. Trying to consider all the facts, he attempted to throw light on the puzzle.

Captain Dunn was the long-time leader of the Rottingdean gang. His sister was the Langborn cook and his source of information. Was she complicit, though?

Colonel Prescott had been the apparent mastermind and insider in the Home Office which allowed him to have foreign connections and influence the number of Revenue men.

The Reverend Howard was new to the area and his family was the most likely source of the arms being exported.

So what—or who—was the link between the three? Was there a link?

How he wished he had Yardley's connections here to look into some possibilities, but it would take weeks, if not months, for a

message to be sent and returned to him. By then, it might be too late—
especially if Dunn was still trailing them.

They had passed through the Strait of Gibraltar and were on the
open seas heading towards Malta.

"Why the furrowed brow?" Harris called from his perch behind
the wheel.

"I am trying to piece together the mystery."

"Any success?" He looked down over the railing to where David
leaned against the ship's side amidst the decks being swabbed to the
refrain of jaunty sea shanties.

"Nay. I am convinced there is a link between Dunn, Prescott and
Howard we have yet to discover." He blew some shavings off into the
water before looking up at Harris.

"Ship approaching full sail about four knots to the west, Cap'n!"
one of the sailors called out. All of the deck-hands immediately
jumped to their feet and took up stations around the ship, awaiting
orders.

Harris took the spy-glass and placed it against his eye.

David watched with anticipation and wariness. He was a fish out
of water if they were attacked at sea. Was Dunn bold enough to give
chase in broad daylight? And would he have the means to do so?
David thought it very unlikely and held up his hand as a shield,
squinting against the sun in an attempt to spot the vessel. To the
untrained eye, it was easy to imagine every wave was a sail or bow...
until it appeared from nowhere, sails at full mast, giving chase.

Once it was close enough to see, Harris put the glass back to his
eye. "It appears to be a British cargo ship," he said, squinting. "By Jove!
It is a Davenport ship, signalling to board!"

Harris handed him the glass and ran up to give orders to allow the
ship to come alongside and prepare to be boarded.

David had never looked through one of these. It magnified everything, and it was unsteadying at first. He scanned back and forth,
seeing nothing but water. He looked away to get his bearings and
tried again before placing it to his eye, only to jump back when he met

with a giant-sized image of Yardley's face, directly in front of him. He tried again, slowly moving the glass to each side.

Scanning the crowd along the railing of the approaching ship, he could discern Cavenray and his Duchess, Yardley and his Duchess, and Letty. Had the entire clan come?

"What on earth are they doing? If they were following to join us on holiday, they would not be racing at such speeds after us," Harris remarked.

"Why did they bring the entire extended family?" David pondered out loud.

"I expect we will find out soon enough," he said, waving as they came closer and into view.

As the crew began to scurry about, furling sails and running up the rigging, Charlotte joined them on the deck. "What is happening? Oh! What are they doing here?"

"I think we are about to find out," David answered as the ships dropped anchor alongside each other and the crews held steady the gangway linking the two ships together.

Yardley crossed first and then handed down his Duchess.

"Charlotte! I am relieved to see you unharmed," the Duke said as he embraced his sister.

Everyone else joined them aboard *The Wind* and made their greetings. David could tell Charlotte was in shock as her face scanned from one to the other.

"Would you care to explain why you thought to find me injured?" Charlotte asked.

"We had planned to follow you in anticipation of a happy event." He coughed to hide his smile. "As to how we managed to catch up with you so quickly, that is another matter. We had arranged to have the younger Captain Harris pick us up at Langborn and proceed at a leisurely pace to Malta once his commission was resigned from the navy. However, when we reached Langborn, we found the place broken into and ransacked. We had given the servants time off, since none of us were in residence, so we do not know precisely when it happened."

Charlotte said nothing, and watched as her brother finished telling the story.

"The areas which had been torn apart were your chambers, your parlour, and the library."

"All the places where I spent my time," she remarked with remarkable composure.

"Which is why we were concerned for your safety, and Davenport was able to provide us with passage immediately. It is too much of a coincidence to assume it was not related to the unfortunate business with Prescott."

"Indeed," David agreed. "Her cabin here was also ransacked last night."

"How did they catch you so swiftly? You must have been followed for some time." Yardley began to pace, his hands behind his back, as everyone else stood and watched with looks of intense concentration on their faces.

"Dunn stowed away in his sister's berth," David explained, "but has since jumped ship, according to your cook."

"Dunn is alive?" Yardley looked stunned and the others were also exclaiming their shock.

"Indeed. None of us saw him, but your cook confirmed he was on board."

"I sent Cook along as a boon to cheer Charlotte. You mean to tell me she aided her brother in these schemes?"

"She did not seem to be fully aware of what he had done. She is in the hold until we decide what to do with her." David removed his hat and wiped the sweat from his brow.

"What can they want from me?" Charlotte spoke up for the first time in a few minutes.

"I have been going over everything, trying to come to that conclusion," David answered.

"I do not know anything! I do not have anything!" she exclaimed with disbelief.

"We now know that Dunn did not die on the yacht that night," Harris said.

"I cannot help but feel there is some connection we are missing between Howard, Prescott and Dunn."

"Is there anything more to be discovered from Cook?" Yardley asked.

"We have exhausted her knowledge, which was minimal."

"Let me fetch my reports on them, and perhaps, if we employ all of our minds, we might piece it together." The Duke left to find the papers, and Jolie, Maili and Cavenray also left to oversee the transference of their belongings to *The Wind*. The rest of them removed to the Captain's dining room, a luxuriously appointed cabin with mahogany panelling and dark green paint. Maps and paintings adorned the walls. The centre of the room held a long wooden table where they sat and waited for him to return.

"You knew Prescott from school, correct?" David asked when they were all seated and Yardley was back with his reports.

Yardley nodded. "As well as Davenport. It is still difficult to believe Prescott was a traitor," Yardley said through clenched teeth.

"Was there anything about him that was unusual? Anything about his family?"

David could see the Duke concentrating. "I never went home with him on a holiday. Perhaps Davenport will be able to tell you more. I cannot recall ever having met his family. One assumes certain things about anyone they are at public school with, you know."

David did know the nobility often assumed all were wealthy. He and Cavenray had been at school together. Being one who was lesser in status, he had always been jealous of those like Cavenray and Yardley who were heirs to great titles and estates. He was not surprised that Yardley had been oblivious to such things as a youth.

"Where is Davenport?" David asked. "I assume he is with you?"

"He is still on the other ship, making arrangements. This was not their usual route and we will need to transfer our possessions so they can continue with their course. I will see if he can come and assist us," Letty answered before leaving the dining room.

"Did anything from your records indicate an association between the three men? Do you know aught of Prescott's army record?"

Yardley began perusing his agent's notes. "There has to be something to link these men."

"Could Dunn also have been in the army at some point? Many men served, especially during the time of Napoleon. It was not so long ago."

"Fairmont or Wyndham would know, if they were here," the Duke muttered.

David watched Yardley attempting to read through pages and pages of documents before him.

"I should have read through these sooner. I merely accepted my agent's word that there was no connection. We stopped looking when we thought Prescott and Dunn were both dead. Then, my only thought was for Charlotte's safety."

"May I look through one of the files while you search the others?" David asked.

"An excellent notion." Yardley handed him Howard's file.

The men read in silence while Charlotte took the third file and also began to read.

"Howard was in the army before he became a man of the cloth!" Charlotte exclaimed.

"Does it say why he left the army?" David asked, frowning.

"No, but it does say he was in the 30th Regiment of Foot and he sold out in 1813."

"Before Waterloo. Is there anything in Dunn's record about having served in the army?" Yardley asked.

"Let me look back that far. He has quite a record of smuggling in here," David remarked.

"Prescott had been at the Home Office for the past decade. There is no note of his Regiment in here," Yardley stated while David continued to search.

Letty returned with Davenport and they quickly told him what they knew. "Prescott was an orphan, a charity student—some pet project of an old dowager. I am surprised you were unaware."

"It never mattered to me," Yardley admitted. "Did he enter the army with a commission?"

"No. He earned his promotions in the field for valour."

"I am not surprised—he was always ambitious. Do you happen to know which Regiment he served in?"

"He enlisted in the 30th Regiment of Foot, but he was moved when he was commissioned."

Charlotte gasped.

"So Prescott and Howard were both in the same Regiment. I am willing to bet Dunn served with them."

"I imagine Cook can verify that," Charlotte said.

"But what happened to make them betray their country?"

"Only Dunn and Howard can answer that. We may not know until we return to question him."

"Let us hope that is not too late."

CHAPTER 21

I have never before considered myself a selfish being, but suddenly I wish everyone to perdition, so I can have Sir David all to myself.—18 April

Charlotte had mixed emotions about everyone joining them. She had been enjoying her time alone with David and was afraid that something would happen to end the fairy tale. It had been several days since her cabin had been rummaged through, so it was easy to pretend it had never happened. She still could not imagine what Dunn could have been looking for, or if he would come back again.

David seemed more relaxed and willing to accept his place amongst her family, though he had not been so openly affectionate since her family had arrived. It was not marked, as if he was unpleasant or rude, he was just more guarded and proper, as though they were back in Society. She hated it. It was somewhat understandable, for she would feel the same way in his position. However, it did not lessen the longing to have that freedom back. Letty and Davenport showed obvious warmth for each other, and they all expected an announcement any day.

They reached Malta on the tenth day of travel without any further incident. The waters were as beautiful as her mother had described, and they could see clear to the sea floor when they sailed close to the shore. There was an imposing, white stone fort and cathedral standing guard over the island, its wall and high towers proclaiming a grand fortress. The entire city was built of the same white rock, and the island was surrounded by the same jagged stone. It felt not of this world.

There was no doubt in Charlotte's mind her mother would be surprised by her visitors. There had not been time to send word and they would see how far her new husband's hospitality stretched. It should not be difficult to find the Villa Pieta in a town of this size. The crew prepared to drop anchor and release the small dinghy boats to row them to the dock. From there, some chairs and donkey carts were hired—there were, of course, no grand carriages awaiting their arrival.

Dusty, pebbled streets were lined with open markets full of fresh fruits, vegetables and flowers, and vendors advertising their goods in English as well as another language. Strange music filled the air as minstrels played on various corners, hoping for a coin as reward. Animals and children ran amok between the patrons, and exotic smells wafted to their noses. The local villagers watched their parade through the town with keen interest and perhaps amusement, as it could well have appeared more like a gypsy caravan than the processional of dukes and duchesses that it was.

Yardley was the first to enter the gates to the Villa and lead the way up a steep stone driveway lined with olive trees. Charlotte had time to take in her surroundings as they waited at a large wooden door for admittance. The house was built of white limestone with a red tile roof and an ornamental balustrade. Boxes of bright pink flowers hung from every window sill, framed by wooden shutters, and a green flowering vine crept up the walls to complete the enchanting picture. A warm breeze from the sea gave relief to the hot afternoon sun. It was not long before her mother bestirred herself and came through the front door to greet them under the portico. A handsome gentleman, somewhat on the portly side with dark hair greying around his temples, followed her. He had deep laughter lines around his eyes and the sides of his mouth, his true character revealed by the twinkle in his eyes. Charlotte loved him on sight.

"You must be my new step-papa, Lord Mompalao-Marquis di Taflia," she said, stepping forward to receive a kiss on each cheek.

He then took her hands and kissed them regally. "Please call me, Vittor. It is much easier on the mouth, no? And you are my new daughter, Charlotte. You are every bit as beautiful as your mama said you were."

David was nearby, but he did not step forward to touch her or introduce himself or make claim to her in any way.

"And who is this handsome fellow? He is your beau, yes?"

Before Charlotte could stutter her embarrassment, David stepped forward and took her arm.

"She is still trying to determine if I am worthy, which, of course, I am not. I hope she will have me nonetheless." He smiled down at her with affection.

The Dowager gasped and clapped her hands with joy and Vittor released a jolly, booming laugh, the rest of the family joining in. She had forgotten their presence. Her cheeks flared with the heat of embarrassment.

"Come inside and let us treat you to proper Maltese hospitality. We are so delighted you are here. I thought we might have to come to England and force you to return with us," he said as he drew her mother to his side and kissed her cheek.

Charlotte could not remember her mother ever looking so happy or vibrant. Charlotte could not be more delighted, though she had expected they would spend her own spinster years together. Her mama had truly found her love and her place. That was what she hoped for with David. Would it ever come to be? It felt as though it was just within her grasp but she could not quite reach it.

The ladies were shown to a drawing room which opened on to a terrace boasting views of a garden and the ocean beyond. They were a sharp contrast to the often dark, rocky and cold views she had at Langborn. Trays of fresh fruits and strange, exotic foods were placed before them—olives, goat's cheeses and fresh bread with thinly sliced ham. Tea was brought, along with fresh-squeezed lemonade.

The men were drawn away to Vittor's study, no doubt to appraise him of the possible threat they still faced. Yardley had sent word back to England, but they might not receive any further information before they returned home themselves.

"Now we may speak freely," her mother said, fanning herself as she settled on a wicker chaise longue covered with cerulean blue pillows. Jolie, Letty, Maili and Charlotte all laughed. "I feel as though I have missed a great deal and I want to hear everything!"

"You have missed a great deal, Mother. However, you are the one who married without any word until after the fact." Charlotte arched a brow in mock reprimand.

The Dowager giggled in response like a young girl in her first Season. Charlotte was stupefied.

"When did you become betrothed?" her mother countered.

"We are not, officially." Charlotte could feel her cheeks flush.

"But he as much as made a declaration on your arrival!" Her mother stretched out her hand towards the front of the house.

"I think, dear Mama, it would be best to explain from the beginning," Jolie interceded. Charlotte gave her a grateful look.

"Several months ago, Sir David Douglas and Miss Dickerson—Letty—returned from the West Indies, where they had been living, in hiding, for a decade."

The Dowager raised her eyebrows but waved her hand for Jolie to continue.

"As a young man, Sir David had been caught up with Lord Brennan in his smuggling schemes and having escaped, had left to protect the Douglas children as well as Letty."

"I heard of Lord Brennan's death before I left England. It was quite a scandal."

"Yes, it was, and because of Uncle David's involvement, he required a pardon from the King," Letty added.

"Which the King refused to give unless Sir David performed for him one more service," Charlotte said.

"That sounds just like our dear George," the Dowager replied.

"He wanted Sir David to capture the leader of the Rottingdean gang."

"Everyone in the vicinity knew they had been operating there for ages without any real harm. What did he want with them?" The Dowager frowned.

"It was discovered they were smuggling arms and munitions to our enemies. They were also using Langborn and Yardley's yacht for their nefarious purposes. Not to mention they killed some of the Revenue Officers."

The Dowager gasped and snatched her hand to her chest in astonishment. Charlotte almost laughed. She had missed her mother's eccentricities.

"Sir David and Yardley were working together, but dear Charlotte uncovered everything. She was almost killed by Colonel Prescott when she discovered them moving goods one night," Jolie added.

"Charlotte, whatever were you thinking?" her mother asked with disbelief.

"I am safe now, Mama."

"I can see that and I can also see you are in love with Sir David. Does this mean everything has turned out for the best? Has he been pardoned?"

Charlotte could do without her mother's bluntness.

"He has been pardoned and has retained the baronetcy and estate. Yardley surprised me by sending him on the ship with me when I was coming to visit you."

"I imagine Yardley had some help with matchmaking." She cast a sly look at Jolie, who only smiled.

"Several nights after we set sail, my cabin was ransacked."

The Dowager shook her head. "Was this a coincidence?"

"We do not think so," Jolie answered. "When we arrived at Langborn to follow them at a leisurely pace, we also found Charlotte's apartments had been rummaged through. We believed she was in danger and followed after them as fast as possible."

"There have been no incidents in several days, Mama. Perhaps he found what he was looking for."

"I certainly hope so! I assume the men will see to our safety here," she said dismissively, as though she could not be bothered to consider that any more danger existed. "I think we should plan a wedding!"

"Mama!"

"Well, you were on a ship with him unchaperoned, and I insist you wed here. You must admit, it is inordinately romantic."

Charlotte cast her gaze to the heavens. She needed some privacy with David, and soon.

DAVID FOUND Charlotte standing on the veranda, alone at last. A self-mocking smile curved his lips as he recalled the first night he had approached her on the terrace—as though drawn to her by some unconscious force.

"Have we come full circle, my lady?" He took her into his arms and spun her about.

Charlotte laughed and it was music to his ears. "I suppose you could say that."

"What do you think of Malta so far? Do you enjoy the island life?"

"I certainly enjoy the warmth and the views. I have never seen anything like it—I feel as if I have walked into a fairy tale."

"You would enjoy Barbados. It is every bit as beautiful as this."

"Perhaps you can take me there, one day." She turned and smiled coyly.

"How can you be so sure, Charlotte?"

"Of you?"

"Yes," he whispered, as he put his arms around her, relishing the comfort of her.

"I just know. Perhaps that is the difference between men and women?" She looked up into his eyes, searching.

"Not entirely. I have always been drawn to you—known you were far too good for me—but men are perhaps more hesitant to come to terms with their innermost feelings."

"I do not believe I care what words you say to me so much as how your actions speak."

"So the words I have been trying to say to you for days no longer matter?" he asked with a devilish look.

She swatted his arm. "I did not say they were not welcome." Her face was adorably exasperated. "Now tell me what you were going to say."

"If you are certain..."

She glared at him.

He took advantage of her prim chin pointing upwards to bend down and cover her lips with his. He could not resist the temptation, so he told her his feelings more eloquently with a kiss than he ever could have done words. Charlotte was receptive—she always had been. She leaned into him and, for the first time, he did not fight his feelings with guilt but embraced the uninhibited love and promise of passion. He had to gather his will to pull away.

"I want to marry you, Charlotte. I want to spend the rest of my days with you. I know it is completely selfish of me to ask, but you seem to want me despite all my faults. And there are many, many faults. Lady Charlotte, will you marry me? Will you have me?"

"I think you know the answer to that," she answered as she pulled his head back down to hers. "I do not wish to wait another day."

Another kiss ensued, and it was some minutes before either were capable of words.

"Would you like to marry here, so your mother can be present? Or would you prefer to wait and have a grand Society wedding?"

"If those are my two choices there is no question. I would much prefer to marry here and quickly."

He chuckled. "Then I will endeavour to make it happen as soon as possible. Am I going to go to the trouble, though, only to find all the duchesses have other plans?"

"A very good question. Why do we not plan it and then just tell them?"

"Another remarkable notion," he mused.

"Now that is resolved, are you going to tell me what you men were discussing for so long this afternoon?"

"I would rather not." He stepped back and ran his hand over his face.

"Has something happened?"

"Nothing has happened, precisely. However, there was a letter waiting here for your brother, from Lord Fairmont."

"What did Nathaniel have to say? I cannot imagine how he got a letter here so soon." She shook her head. "I suppose if anyone could it would be he."

"I imagine he sent it express courier across the Continent. Your brother had asked him to continue investigating once he found your home had been searched. Reverend Howard was a fount of information under Fairmont's interrogation."

"Did he discover something?"

"He confirmed what we suspected. The three men all enlisted as privates in the 30th Regiment of Foot. Their battalion commander had them publicly flogged—for atrocities I would prefer not to repeat to a lady's ears—after Badajoz, and they have carried a grudge to this day. It took significant digging to discover more information on Prescott, however."

"Yes, he was a Colonel and remained in the army."

"All the better to carry out his grudge, I suspect. Apparently, the officer in question had turned and run from the fighting. Prescott found him hiding at Salamanca. He later blackmailed this man to get the promotions and worm his way into the Home Office."

Charlotte closed her eyes and blew out a breath of astonishment. "Yes, it all begins to make sense. It does not justify their actions, but I have never been in such a situation. From Nathaniel's stories, war was quite horrific."

"I think there are many layers to this," David said in a measured way. "The enlisted ranks did not have it easy. Most of the time there were not enough rations, shoes were inadequate, and feet were blistered after marching for miles each day...pay was not reliable. There was often resentment of their superiors—and if you throw an arrogant coward into the mix, it is a disaster. It is easy to forget what you are fighting for without an honourable leader."

"I suppose it makes it a little easier to understand now that I know the how and why, but it still does not explain why they are continuing to come after me, or at least my belongings."

"No, I know." He pulled her back into his arms and she rested her head on his shoulder. They began to sway back and forth; and David never wanted to let her go. He wanted to keep her safe in his arms forever.

CHAPTER 22

If something seems too good to be true, it is.—21 April

The blessed day had finally arrived. Charlotte could not believe it was actually happening. David had arranged everything from the church to the Reverend and the time, and had allowed the other ladies to arrange the breakfast at the villa afterwards. Their small party were the only guests, but she supposed the family wanted it to be as special as possible. Charlotte only wanted to be Mrs. Douglas—or Lady Douglas, as it would properly be. It was all she had wanted since the moment he first spoke to her. The rest mattered little.

It was a warm morning and as she rode through the streets of Valletta to St. Peter's Cathedral in an open landau, she held a small bouquet of lilies and roses to her nose. She inhaled; their sweet scent mixed with the sea air and smells of fresh baking in nearby kitchens to fill her heart with simple joy. Pretending not to notice the armed guards in front and behind them, she refused to allow thoughts of that horrid man to intrude upon her wedding day. When they arrived at the church, Yardley helped her alight and led her up the steps to the wooden front doors. It looked much like one of the grand cathedrals at home, with its tower and dome holding court majestically above the rest of the town. Inside, he led her down the aisle through the nave, its inside reflecting the bright sunshine from without, the stained glass windows casting a rainbow of colours across the church.

Sir David was waiting for her at the altar, looking more handsome than she had ever seen. Freshly shaven, with his dark hair combed back, he was dressed in grey trousers and coat, a silver waistcoat and a white neckcloth. He looked divine.

Her own gown was one of the new creations she had yet to wear, a pomona green silk the same shade as her eyes. For once, she truly believed the notion that beauty shone from the inside out, for she felt happy and knew it was bursting from her. The look on David's face when he took her hand from Yardley's was all she needed as proof.

The ceremony was brief and to the point, though she did appreciate the fact their marriage was sealed in a church, performed by a bishop. She had signed a register and would have a British marriage license. It was real. Happiness felt like it was finally within her grasp— especially when David looked at her as though she were the only woman in the world.

They returned to the villa and were joined by some of her stepfather's family for the celebration. The feasting and dancing continued well into the evening. Charlotte's feet hurt and she was ready to escape with David. She did not know if it would be rude to say their goodbyes and retire for the evening. Unfortunately, they could not go away, since there was nowhere else to go. Charlotte took a few moments to herself on the terrace, to watch the sunset while waiting for David to join her at what had become their special place. She was going to miss this magical feeling of eternal summer. Now that her mother had settled here, they would have reason to visit often.

They were returning to England soon to start their new life together. Yardley felt that it was necessary for them to present themselves in Society with the full support of Cavenray, Craig, Harris, Wyndham and everyone else they could gather to present a united front. She also wished to attend the wedding of Mr. Davenport to Letty, who did not wish to wed without her mother's presence.

Inhaling the fresh scent of pelargoniums, which filled the boxes surrounding the terrace, she stayed outside, lost in her musings about her wedding night and what the future would hold for them as a married couple.

One large hand gripped her arm as another hand clamped over her mouth. Her nostrils filled with the smells of unwashed sweat and rancid breath. "I knew I would eventually find you. Now, if you promise not to scream, I'll take my hand off your mouth."

After nodding her agreement, he dropped his hand. A vice-like grip took hold of her heart and squeezed it. She did not know the voice, but it was not a friendly one. The cool blade of a knife pressed upwards against her throat. She swallowed hard, despite her most fervent wish to remain still. Charlotte knew if she turned her head to look it would be Captain Dunn. How had he managed to pass the guards?

"Aren't ye going to say something?"

"What do you want from me?" Her voice trembled.

He cackled; it was a frightening sound one could scarce call a laugh. "What do I want? I want my life back. Ye took that from me. Ye realize that, don't ye?"

"I thought you died," she said softly.

"Would that I had." He forced her head sideways to look at his scarred face. She had not seen him often enough to have memorized his features, but she could tell he had been badly burned. Raw, puckered flesh pulled in tight lines against his jaw, and beady black eyes watched her with a challenge in their crow-like depths. "I jumped in the water before it got the rest 'o me."

She kept her gaze steady, refusing to show fright. It would hardly be appropriate to voice her thoughts on the fact that she wished she had shot him instead of the boat.

"Well, here we are, Mr. Dunn. What do you intend now?"

"You are a cold fish. Not at all what I expected from what Edna said." Edna was his sister—her cook, the snitch.

"I am sorry if I disappoint you, sir," she said in her haughtiest tone.

195

"I actually like ye, Lady Charlotte. I tell ye what. I will make ye a deal. I will let ye live if ye hand it over."

"I know not of what you search for, sir. I would be delighted to give you what you seek if you will only enlighten me as to its nature," she said, hoping her voice sounded steadier than it felt.

"'Twould be a shame if I had to make yer face look like mine. Or better yet, do something to that double-dealing husband of yers."

"I am in earnest, Mr. Dunn. I have no idea what it is you want."

He spat in her face and it was all she could do not to retch. He was about to lose patience with her and she knew she was running out of time. She had been gone for some time now. Why were they not looking for her?

"Now ye are going to lead me to yer chambers without being seen. Then ye are going to hand it over and we will part friendly-like and ye will forget ye ever saw me. Understood?"

She gave a slight nod, still very conscious of the blade pressed to her throat.

"You will be much more noticeable holding me like this. I promise to walk with you without a fuss."

"Very well, but if you yell I will slit your throat and then find your husband and kill him." He released the blade from her throat and she turned to enter the house. She chose the farthest door on the terrace away from the dancing.

Looking through the door before entering, she motioned for him to follow. It was frighteningly easy to pass through the house unnoticed. There were no servants in this wing since they were all attending to the wedding feast.

When they reached her chambers, entirely too soon, he closed the door and locked it behind her.

"Now, what can I provide for you, Mr. Dunn? I know it is not jewels, since you did not take them from my cabin on the ship, and I cannot conjecture what else of value I have that you would want."

"I didn't say I didn't want your jewels. In fact, they will come in handy, since I had the added expense of coming all this way after you. What I'm looking fer is worth more than yer trinkets."

She walked to her dressing table and opened the drawer, pulling out a pouch of jewels and with it a small knife she had hidden there. She tossed him the pouch and then proceeded to hide the knife in the folds of her skirt while he was distracted. "How did you manage to follow the ship?" She thought to keep him talking and satisfy her curiosity at the same time.

"I stowed in my sister's cabin until the night I searched yers. Thought you'd never leave it, I did."

"And then? If you had not made a mess I would have been none the wiser." She also unwound the pearl necklace she was wearing.

"I got impatient and heard someone coming. Had to swim te shore and find passage on a fishin' boat. Now, hurry up."

"I would prefer to keep my wedding ring," she said as she handed the pearls over, hoping he did not notice the blade trembling in her other hand.

"Very generous of you, my lady." He made a mocking bow. "Now I want the key."

"The key?" Disbelief must have shone on her face and through her voice.

"Too much blue blood makes you daft in the head, you know." He sneered.

"I beg your pardon! There is no need to insult me."

"Begging your forgiveness, my lady," he said in a most sarcastic voice. "Everybody knows about the hidden treasure in the Langborn caves. It's said the key to the map is hidden in an heirloom passed down from generation to generation amongst the ladies of the family. When ye marry, ye pass it on to the next. So I mean to 'ave it afore ye pass it on."

Charlotte could not think of what he was referring to. The only thing she had been given was an old hairbrush from her grandmother. She shook her head. "I am sorry, I do not have what you seek."

He growled with frustration and lunged at her. In the same instant, she heard someone yell her name. She jumped back and barely escaped his grasp.

"Charlotte! Charlotte! Open the door!" The anguished demand

was followed by a hand rattling the latch and a fist pounding at the door.

She looked from the door to Dunn, uncertain how to handle this occurrence and keep herself from being eviscerated.

"I do not have what you seek. Leave by the window. You have my jewels. I will tell no one," she said in a loud whisper. There was the sound of wood splintering as heavy crashes began to shake the door.

"I am afraid it is too late for that," David announced, bursting into the room as the door fell from its hinges.

Dunn's demeanour changed, his eyes taking on a look of possession, and he growled at David, who rushed past her to corner the other man. They were going to exchange blows, she could sense it, but David did not have a weapon.

Charlotte knew what he was doing—trying to deflect his attention from her, but she could not allow him to sacrifice himself. She gripped the knife hidden under the folds of her skirt and stepped in between the two men. With a ferocious bellow, Dunn lunged forward and grabbed her.

 ***

Dunn seized Charlotte's wrist and wrenched her around in front of him. Within a heartbeat, a blade was at her throat and David prayed he could do what he needed to do without hurting her. She looked up to meet his gaze; her sweet face was filled with desperation.

David's heart pounded inside his chest. How could she sacrifice herself? Dunn would slice her with the knife he held at her neck before she could blink. He wanted to scream at the wrongness of it, but it was too late.

"Let her go, Dunn. It is me you want."

"Ye know what I want."

"I do not have what you seek, and you have enough jewels there to set you up in a new place for a goodly while," she said calmly, though her voice shook.

"No, my lady. I am afraid I cannot do that. There is nothing left for me without the key. I need to be set up for the rest of my life, not a while. Where do you think I can start again, looking like this?"

"I will give you a place to make a new start. Just let her go," David commanded with as much authority as he could.

"'Ow could I trust ye?" He shook his head. "I can't. Now step back out of the room and leave or the lady dies." He shoved her forward, the blade pricking through her skin.

David saw nothing save red fury. Dunn would pay for harming Charlotte.

He looked at her and her eyes lowered to her trembling hand, nestled against her skirts. She was holding a knife! He did not know if she could wield it hard enough to do any damage, but he knew she was going to try something. She stared straight at him, her intention clear; she knew she could not let Dunn take her. Blood began to run down her neck. Dunn was gripping her with such force she was struggling to breathe. Heedless, the scoundrel began to drag her towards the balcony door. David knew at once, if Dunn was allowed to leave with her, then his own chances of saving his wife were nil.

Courageous girl, she was dragging her feet, resisting as much as possible. Somehow—it could only be by God's good grace—she yet avoided her slender neck being sliced further. *Have a care, my love!*

"Move, now!" Dunn demanded.

David took a small step sideways as Dunn released one hand to lift the latch on the balcony door. Charlotte took her chance. She thrust her dagger into his leg with a wild screech. As Dunn yelped in pain, David took his opportunity and attacked.

He leaped forward, pushing Dunn away from Charlotte and wrestling him to the ground. The blade spun away across the floor, out of reach.

"Go for help, Charlotte!" he commanded as he dodged a blow.

He saw her tugging frantically at the bell-pull before she ran to the bed, searching feverishly for something. It was difficult to watch her while struggling with Dunn. She removed the cord holding back the hangings and hurried to his side.

"No, Charlotte!"

Ignoring him, she tried to grab Dunn's feet as they fought. Dunn was fighting like a man who knew it was his last stand. She grabbed

ELIZABETH JOHNS

one of his legs and held on as he kicked. That gave David the advantage and he managed to land Dunn a facer, rendering him still. The dagger was still sticking out of his leg, the wound inflicted bleeding over the carpet at an alarming rate. David knew he could not live long with so much blood loss. He took the cord and tied Dunn's hands.

David's chest flailed up and down, his breathing hard as he rose to his feet. Charlotte ran into his arms. Although he needed to go for help, he could not let her go.

"Hush, it is over now. He cannot hurt you any more," he said as he held her and reassured her. Taking the cloth from the wash-basin, he pressed it over her neck. He then kissed the top of her head and removed his neckcloth before removing the knife and tying it around Dunn's leg. "I do not know if it will stop the blood flow, or whether it is for the best to try and save his life. It is doubtless futile, either way." He put pressure on the leg, regardless of his words.

"It is in God's hands now," she agreed, fetching a basin of water in order to help.

A footman came rushing in at that moment. Pausing in the doorway, he paled at the sight before him.

"Send for a doctor and ask for the gentlemen to come quickly."

"Yes, sir!" The young man hurried away.

It was not long before a crowd of gentlemen and servants were upon them.

"What has happened?" Yardley demanded as he took in the situation. He let out an oath when his gaze went from Dunn to Charlotte. "You are bleeding!"

"Only a scratch," she replied, though David could feel her trembling.

Yardley bent down to assess Dunn. "He will not be with us long at the rate he is bleeding. The doctor should be here shortly."

"I will stay with him," Lord Harris offered. "Take Charlotte away from this."

"An excellent thought. Come with me and we will soon settle your nerves, my lady."

David scooped her up into his arms before she could protest.

There was no better sensation than the relief that this was over. He placed her on a sofa in one of the family parlours, and the women at once descended, like a bees in a hive, to fuss over her.

"Here, Lottie, this will settle your nerves." Yardley handed her a glass of brandy and she looked at David and smiled, clearly remembering the last time she had used spirits to calm herself. "Only one small sip," she said demurely.

"At least we are married now," he whispered in her ear, deliberately infusing his tone with a hint of things to come.

"Thank God," she replied, looking up at him with the most glorious smile ever bestowed upon him.

Although everyone was talking and fussing around them, they largely ignored those present. For the moment, no one else existed but the two of them. Hopefully, David thought, their relations would take the hint and leave them alone.

He knew explanations would be necessary before he could have Charlotte to himself, but he intended to savour every precious moment he had with her. Tonight had been a close-run thing—too close by half. He tightened his hold on her and kissed the top of her head. He liked kissing her hair; it was so soft and sweet-smelling.

Harris came into the parlour. "Dunn has died."

"Good riddance," David muttered.

"Did he say what he was looking for?" Jolie asked Charlotte.

"Yes, but he seemed to be labouring under a delusion. He was looking for an heirloom that is passed down from generation to generation. He said it holds a hidden key to a treasure map. I could not convince him he was mistaken. The only thing I have is Grandmother Yardley's hairbrush."

"Oh, my dear," her mother said. "The brush." She sent one of the servants to fetch it.

When the maid returned with the brush, her mother slid away the back, revealing a hidden compartment...which was empty.

"How disappointing," Charlotte remarked.

"There has long been an old wives' tale of treasure hidden in the Langborn caves—all just a myth, of course. No doubt it began as a bedtime story, concocted for a mischievous Yardley ancestor. I had quite forgotten about the brush. It was never mine, for it came to you from your grandmother Yardley."

"If she told me about the compartment I have forgotten," Charlotte said, squinting as though she were trying to remember. I was very young when it came into my possession. It is time to pass it on to your eldest daughter, Benedict. There will be lots more stories to pass on with it now," she added dryly.

Everyone in the room chuckled, the laughter a welcome reprieve from the strain.

"If you do not mind, I think I will take Charlotte to rest. If we are needed to speak to the magistrate, you know where to find us, but it is our wedding day, after all." He winked at her, wickedly enjoying her fiery blush of response.

"That will not be necessary. I will take care of everything," Vittor said.

"Thank you," David replied, and without further ado, he carried his wife away to help her forget the evils of the world.

EPILOGUE

Life is sweeter than I could ever have dreamed it would be. It is not easy, but victory is more rewarding having had to work for it. I might have regained a pound or two, but David seems to like me with a fuller figure. I have three beautiful children to show for it and I have finally learned to embrace myself —just as I am.—15 May 1835

"Look, Papa! Do you like it?" Young Nigel held up the evidence of his handiwork to show David.

It was a simple fish but the boy was showing promise of having inherited his father's talents.

"I think yours looks better than mine," David said as he held up his own carving to compare with his son's.

"Land ahoy!" the bosun shouted and they all hurried to starboard to see what they had waited weeks for. Charlotte held young baby Kate on one hip, while Thomas held onto her other as he tried to climb the railing to see what everyone else could see. The island in the distance bore small mountains lush with green vegetation. The ship skirted rocky cliffs in some places and white sandy beaches in others.

"I thought we would never see land again," Charlotte laughed with relief.

"The trip will be worth it, I promise."

When they finally docked, they were greeted by crystal clear turquoise waters and thick, warm air, the occasional scent of unusual spices roasting on meat wafting through the breeze. They followed David as he walked up the incline to his property. With his arms spread wide, he spun about laughing. "Here we are! This is Sugar Grove Plantation!"

Charlotte paused to allow the warm breeze to blow in her face and inhale the fresh scents of pine trees and other unfamiliar fragrances. When she opened her eyes, she looked around to memorize every feature of this incredible place. David was pointing some unusual trees out to Nigel and Thomas.

"These are palm trees. Do you see the round brown balls at the top?" David pointed a finger to where three balls hung between the leaves.

"I see them, Papa!" The little boys jumped up and down, exclaiming in glee.

"Those are coconuts. Later I will cut one open for you and you can drink the milk from it."

"I thought milk came from cows and goats, Papa?" Thomas frowned adorably. Charlotte wanted to kiss the wrinkles away but they were gone before she could bend over.

"Milk comes from many different places, son," David explained. "This milk tastes a little different, a little sweeter—but that is a treat for later. Fruit grows everywhere in Barbados. First, we must greet some old friends."

Charlotte followed David's smile to where a group of people were coming briskly towards them.

"Massa David? Is that you?"

David let go of Nigel's hand and throwing his arms around an older woman, picked her up.

She laughed, revealing a toothless grin.

"You're still shameless, I see. Now put me down and introduce me to your family. I 'spect they are better behaved than you."

David laughed, a deep hearty sound. Charlotte was more in love with him than ever. It was still hard to believe he had chosen her. She could not help but beam as David introduced her and their three young children to his workers, who maintained the plantation. A large native family lived there and worked the land.

"Charlotte, this is Seyla. She kept me in order all those years."

"I have no doubt that was quite a task." Charlotte smiled.

"It was my pleasure. Let us go inside," Seyla said. "I can' wait to show you the new house."

"It looks perfect," Charlotte remarked as she gazed up at the white, three-storeyed stuccoed home with a red-tiled roof and sea-green shutters. An ornamental balustrade led up the front steps and surrounded the portico. Palm trees guarded the house and welcomed them with their swaying branches.

"Who would like to have tamarind balls and fresh tea biscuits?" Seyla asked. Two small boys were quickly jumping up and down with excitement.

"I want tea biscuits, please. I do not know what tama balls are," Nigel explained.

"You will know in a moment."

Nurse took the children to the nursery, along with some of the women, to be with some of the plantation children. After being on a ship without other children for so many weeks, Nigel and Thomas were delighted to have friends to play with.

David led her to their suite of rooms and out through the doors on to the balcony.

"I could become accustomed to this. It is every bit as beautiful as I had imagined. Why did you wait so long to bring me here?"

David looked down at her, amusement evident in his gaze.

"We have been a mite busy, between establishing the stud and your bearing three children, my love."

She sighed, allowing a contented smile to spread across her face. "Yes. Dido and Gulliver gave us a wonderful start. Their Apollo and Artemis, along with Minerva and Hector's Astyanax, have given our farm as much work as our home."

"Our horses cannot have more fun than we do," he said with a teasing nudge.

Ignoring his flirtations, she continued, "It also allowed time for a house to be built on the property again."

"True, though it is not as grand as the last one, but since it is not our primary residence, it will do."

"It is perfect. I think we could stay here a while."

He laughed. "Come now, it is not so horrible at Crossings."

"No, I have been quite content there. However, we are here now and I do not want to set foot on a ship for a good, long time."

"Then I shall have to be content here, I suppose," he said in husky tones, wrapping his arms around her from behind and nuzzling her neck.

"Mm," she agreed, somewhat mindlessly. Her wits were struggling to concentrate on his words. He turned her in his arms, his lips devouring hers, and she decided concentrating was overrated.

AFTERWORD

Author's note: British spellings and grammar have been used in an effort to reflect what would have been done in the time period in which the novels are set. While I realize all words may not be exact, I hope you can appreciate the differences and effort made to be historically accurate while attempting to retain readability for the modern audience.

Thank you for reading *Moon and Stars*. I hope you enjoyed it. If you did, please help other readers find this book:

1. This ebook is lendable, so send it to a friend who you think might like it so she or he can discover me, too.
2. Help other people find this book by writing a review.
3. Sign up for my new releases at www.Elizabethjohnsauthor.com, so you can find out about the next book as soon as it's available.
4. Come like my Facebook page www.facebook.com/Elizabethjohnsauthor or follow on Twitter @Ejohnsauthor or feel free to write me at elizabethjohnsauthor@gmail.com

ACKNOWLEDGMENTS

There are many, many people who have contributed to making my books possible.

My family, who deals with the idiosyncrasies of a writer's life that do not fit into a 9 to 5 work day.

Dad, who reads every single version before and after anyone else— that alone qualifies him for sainthood.

Wilette, who takes my visions and interprets them, making them into works of art people open in the first place.

Karen, Tina, Staci, Judy, and Kristiann who care about my stories enough to help me shape them before everyone else sees them.

Heather who helps me say what I mean to!

And to the readers who make all of this possible.
I am forever grateful to you all.

Made in the USA
Middletown, DE
27 June 2020

11109590R00130